A PLAY ON WORDS

A PLAY ON WORDS

Stories, Verses and Plays for the Classroom and Beyond

Barry Gray

Copyright © 2008 by Barry Gray.
Cover art sand painting by Jan Peterson
Cover photography by Ursula Heller

Library of Congress Control Number:	2008906202
ISBN: Hardcover	978-1-4363-5702-9
Softcover	978-1-4363-5701-2

All rights reserved. No part of this book may be reproduced or transmitted in any form or by any means, electronic or mechanical, including photocopying, recording, or by any information storage and retrieval system, without permission in writing from the copyright owner.

This is a work of fiction. Names, characters, places and incidents either are the product of the author's imagination or are used fictitiously, and any resemblance to any actual persons, living or dead, events, or locales is entirely coincidental.

This book was printed in the United States of America.

To order additional copies of this book, contact:
Xlibris Corporation
1-888-795-4274
www.Xlibris.com
Orders@Xlibris.com
50326

A PLAY ON WORDS

An English Language Play by Barry Gray

We are the words of the great English tongue.
Without us you're quiet, you're silent, you're dumb.
We give you the power to com-mun-i-cate.
Without us you can't phone to say you'll be late.

Without us "I love you" just stays in your mind.
You can't shout a warning to someone who's blind.
You can't tell a joke and you can't sing a song.
You maybe can hum, but not whisper along.

Imagine just what we would sound like to you
If you didn't know words and what each one can do.
We'd just be a jumble of meaningless sounds,
Like blah, blah, blahblahblah, blahblahblah, blah, blah.

And not only talking, but writing as well.
Without us, poor people, there's nothing to spell.
No newspapers, magazines, brochures or books,
No columns, no letters, no notes stuck in nooks.

How can you describe a dark crimson sky?
Or tell the whole truth or a tiny white lie?
How can you cut in with your ifs, ands and buts?
How could you send e-mails to castles or huts?

You need all us words, whether spoken or writ,
From the polysyllabic to the tiny word "it."
We know you can speak, you can read, you can write,
But give us a moment, we'll shine a bright light,

On the why's and the wherefores that all teachers teach,
As we try to explain all the main parts of speech.
We'll tell you of adjectives, pronouns and verbs
That are used by the wordsmiths for poems and blurbs.

We'll share all the secrets of adverbs and nouns,
That are much more than just a collection of sounds.
We'll let prepositions, conjunctions and such,
Describe what they do, if it isn't too much.

But who should go first as our story we share?
Who's most important? I don't think we dare
To say one part is better or one part is worse.
We all do our duty in prose and in verse.

So let's toss a coin and we'll see who goes first.
That's how we'll decide . . . .

(*Verbs interrupt, elbow their way to the front*)

CAUTION, VERBS AT WORK!

Nouns are just things, oh, like peanuts or wings,
Adjectives only describe.
Pronouns and articles think they're the kings
Of the whole parts of speech tribe.

But who does the work when it needs to be done?
Certainly not prepositions.
Just call on us verbs and we'll come at a run,
Ready to take up positions.

D'you want to hear some of the ways we can act?
Listen, we'll tell you a few.
None of what follows is false, it's all fact.
These are the things we can do.

We can think, we can eat, we can drink, we can cheat,
We can hollow a log for a drum.
We can navigate, complicate, instigate, meet.
We can awe with our wit, or play dumb.

We can rap, trap or clap, we can flap, snap or grapple
With problems that no-one can solve.
We can peel any fruit from banana to apple.
We change, we advance, we evolve.

Those are things we can do, you should see what we've done,
We've taught all those teachers to teach.
We've lifted, we've broken, we've lost and we've won.
We've boosted, so children can reach.

We dug, sat and rested, we stopped to inquire,
We ate, drank and swallowed it all.
We conquered, we bested, we said you're a liar,
We dialled and gave you a call.

What of things yet to do in the future to come?
We'll be ready to tackle each job.
We will plan, we'll deliver, we'll hollow that drum,
We'll beat on it making it throb.

Do you understand now that without us you're cooked?
You can't do a thing on your own.
So call us and tell us what we've overlooked.
We'll even assist you to phone.

(Everybody except the Verbs)

Come on you guys let's do this fair,
You're always butting in.
You're always so choleric with
Your stuck out, jutting chin.

Let's let the adverbs have their turn,
Because they modify,
You verbs who simply can't sit still.
They'll tell us how and why.

(Interjections rush out and shout . . .)

INTERJECTIONS: Wait!

(Verbs manhandle Interjections back to group)

INTERJECTIONS: But! Ouch! Hey!

(Verbs return to chorus, Adverbs step out and wistfully begin)

HOWARD'S HOW WORDS

(The Adverb's Story)

My name is Howard Helper and I live inside a book,
And if you have a moment I'll show you how I look.

I like to walk so slowly through the meadow green and wide,
While the cows are mooing lowly with their calves close by their side.
I like to run so lightly on a sunny, summer day,
While the sun is shining brightly on the hills across the bay.

I like to saunter carelessly with all my thoughts adrift,
Or tread my way quite fearlessly through chasm, gorge and rift.
I like to plod so steadily up hills so steep and long
And I'll always wait quite readily just to listen to the song
Of the birds that sing so sweetly sitting high up in a tree,
Or of crickets chirping neatly; is their sweet song just for me?

I like to wander aimlessly from here to there and back,
And my time I squander shamelessly along a well-worn track.
I like to prowl cunningly for no one else but me.
Or tight-rope walk quite stunningly for all the world to see.

Perambulating broadly through many different lands,
Or strolling with my darling oh so happily holding hands.
I like to help all doing words explain just how they do
The things that they are doing, things like thinking, reading, chewing,
Clapping, cheering, even booing.
Things like sleeping, dreaming, snoring, they can get so downright boring
If they do not have a helping word, the kind that you've all surely heard,
That tell us how these things are done:
Like brilliantly polished and rapidly run.

If your action words are lonely and they need a little help,
You only have to call me and I'll come at your first yelp.
Veering widely, sneering snidely, rushing rashly, talking brashly.
Touching caringly, climbing daringly, smashing violently, creeping silently.
Rolling roundly, sleeping soundly, staring blankly, speaking frankly.
Thinking clearly, liking dearly,
Expanding increasingly, striving unceasingly.

So there you have my how words, only one more thing to tell:
If you do decide to use them, by all means please use them well.

(Before anything else can happen the Interjections rush out with quick shouts)

INTERJECTIONS: Hey! Watch out! Look!

(Verbs retrieve them to the chorus)

(All reassemble for choral recitation)

Okay now we've seen all the doing that's done.
But who does the doing, the walk, skip or run?
What falls off a cliff or what stands in the way?
Who sings that sad song and who pitches that hay?

There's got to be something or someone who'll do,
All that doing those blustery verbs say they do.
Let's let them explain with their own soothing sounds.
But listen up well because you, too, are nouns. *(pointing at the audience)*

(The group softly encourages the shy Nouns to go front and centre)

NOUNS

Nouns, clowns, towns, gowns, frowns, sounds, mounds, hounds.
Ships, tips, lips, hips, chips, flips, snips, clips.
Dogs, clogs, fogs, bogs, hogs, cogs, frogs, logs.
Bills, chills, drills, hills, spills, grills, pills, frills.
Jacks, slacks, sacks, packs, antique, precious knick-knacks.

All the things of our world are the things we can touch,
We can smell, we can see, we can hear, they're so much
A big part of our lives in and out, day by day
That without them we surely would wander astray.

They're our signposts, our guides, they're the things that we hold.
They're our backpacks, our notebooks, our silver, our gold.
They're the things that we grasp in the palm of our hand.
They're the chair where we sit, they're the floor where we stand.

They're the names of the things that we think of the most.
Names like apple and orange and pillar and post.
But not all of our nouns are from stuff of the Earth.
There's a noun such as death, there's a noun such as birth.

Feelings, dealings, healings, fun, laughter, trust or setting sun.
Courage, pride or awful pain, happiness despite the rain.
Love and glee and joy sans end, loyalty to one's best friend.
Sisters, brothers, parents, pals, aunts and uncles, guys and gals.

So you see that our nouns are a manifold lot.
They're as heavy as rock, they're as light as a thought.
They're the names of all things, as I've told you before,
But they're also the names of the ones we adore.

Names like Mommy and Daddy and Jackie and Jill.
Names like Joseph and Mary and Bonnie and Bill.
Or of places like London or Lima, Peru,
Or like Westminster Abbey or Calgary Zoo.

Names of people and places are called proper nouns.
Their initials are big or you'll soon see the frowns
Of the teachers and wordsmiths and editors, too,
Who are watching the language of me and of you.

That's enough about nouns, now we know that they're names,
So let's sharpen our pencils and play some word games.

(The chorus calls the Nouns back while reciting the following)

No, wait till we introduce all of the parts.
Let's finish the work before the play starts.
We'll show you the words who are made to assist.
They bring in that colour, they give it that twist.

WE ADJECTIVES

Some people call us colour words, some say that we describe,
But teachers call us adjectives and put us right beside
The naming words which, with our help, must not so boring be,
Like luscious grass and azure glass and blue, blue, shiny sea.

A tree without our help is simply nothing but a tree,
But we can make it tall or short or grandiose or free.
That same old tree is great or proud or stately as a queen,
Or gnarled, weathered, bent or bowed or red or brown or green.

Good boys, fun toys, hot nights, bright lights, deep holes or wide, wide streams.
Brown dogs, fat hogs, steep hills, cold chills, dry lips or scary dreams.
We take those simple naming words, or nouns as teachers say,
And make them salty, sweet or sour, or pink, chartreuse or grey.

We're joyous, happy, light or glum, we're awesome, gruesome, bad.
We're red, we're white, we're black, we're dumb, we're nifty, cool or sad.
So use us please whene'er you speak and also when you write.
The language that you give the world will be a glowing light.

(Chorus)

Wow, that was pretty, oh so nice,
You make those nouns stand out.
So whose turn is it to step up
And all their duties spout?

(Interjections make a move to go out and interject, but the Verbs stop them)

STANDING IN

(The Pronoun's Story)

Sometimes a noun's too cumbersome to speak repeatedly.
Sometimes our mouths can blunder some when wanting to be free
Of repetition, reproduction, duplication, too.
When that's the case, why not erase
Those full grown nouns, long-winded sounds,
And in their place, with scarce a trace
Of largeness, bigness, magnitude,
We'll use some words, as light as birds,
That mean the same as words that name,
Like "it" and "she" and "you."

"It" stands for tree, geography, for elephant and pearl.
"It" stands for almost everything that's not a boy or girl.
A girl's "she," a boy is "he" or sometimes "her" or "him."
Yes, "she" and "he" are standing in for Susan and for Tim.

We're pronouns and we take the place of nouns of any size.
There's "we" and "us" and "they" and "them," we hope you realize,
That with us gone your sentences would very clumsy be
And you would have to use big words instead of "I" and "me."

Susan went to the beach. Susan had a good swim.
Tim lent Susan his towel. Susan said thanks to Tim.
Susan went to the beach and she had a good swim.
Tim lent her his towel and then she thanked him.

Without us it's so difficult to make a sentence flow.
It's "you" and "me" and "her" and "him," we think you ought to know,
A word like "insecurity" can just be said with "it."
So be secure and use pronouns, you'll find they usually fit.

We can also be possessive, we can say that it is "mine."
"My" hand, "your" eyes, "his" cheeks, "her" lies, there's even "thou" and "thine."
We hope you see what pronouns do, they make your language smooth.
So use us well, he, she and it, and make those long nouns move.

Chorus

Who's left to tell their story?
Who hasn't had their say?
Which parts of speech are yet to speak,
To finish up this play?
Who ties it all together?
Who acts like sentence glue?
Of course it's the Conjunctions,
"Cause binding's what they do.

IFS, ANDS AND BUTS

(The conjunction's story)

We join, we bind, we tie, we link,
We're welders, we connect.
We hook up sentence clauses with
The skill that you'd expect,

From words much bigger than us squirts,
With letters less than four.
Like "if" and "and" and "as" and "but"
And "yet" and "or" and "nor."

Sometimes we are much bigger,
"Either," "neither" and "although."
"Because," "unless" or "since" or "while"
To use us you must know,

That we're conjunctions and we do
The job that only we
Can do because that's what we do
For reasons that must be.

INTERJECTIONS: Well! Pssst! Whew! Alas! Oh!

PREPOSITION POSITION

(The Preposition's Story)

Verbs are doers, nouns are things, adverbs tell us *how* she sings.
Adjectives describe like mad, interjections are just bad.
Prepositions, hey that's us, tell you where to steer the bus.
We're the ones who give direction: toward, behind, beside that section.

We're the ones who point the way: above, below, beyond that bay.
Against, ahead, along, among: we guide you all, both old and young.
Into, onto, up and down; we will get you through the town.
Where it's going, where it is; true position is our biz.

ARTICLES

There aren't many of us, but our role you'll soon see.
Our numbers are few, in fact we're just three.
We're Articles and we're the smallest of words,
But our duties are definite, not for the birds.

The definite article simply is "the."
The dog and the cat and the snoring Grandpa.
Indefinite is the most tiny word "a."
It's only one letter, but we like it, yah!

A donkey, a monkey, a warty black toad.
A dumptruck, a toadstool, a long winding road.
But if the next word has the sound of a vowel,
You'd better use "an," or the teachers will howl.

An osprey, an eagle, an ugly black toad,
An orange and green truck with an overweight load.
So there you now see all the articles three,
We're "a," "an," and "the" who we sometimes call "thee."

Chorus

But nobody talks all in rhythm and rhyme.
We don't have the energy, money or time!
We mix up the parts and we each play our role,
And give you a language with heart and with soul.

The individual Parts of Speech now mingle and form rows each according to its role in the sentence. Article, adjective, noun, etc., create sentences such as the following.

The warty, black toad hid quietly under a leaf and slept.

Bring me a ripe banana quickly or I will get angry!

Behind the school an ancient maple tree is fluttering its leaves softly in the breeze.

This is an opportunity for the children to get creative and compose their own sentences using as many parts of speech as possible.

CHORUS *(No longer separated into parts)*

So there all you wonderful people listening out there in the audience, this is what we really sound like in our day-to-day talking. Everything gets mixed up. Some sentences don't use all the parts. Others get pretentious and try to incorporate vast amounts of flowery phrases, interspersed with seemingly unnecessary embellishment used only for the dubious purposes of intending to impress less sophisticated users of the language. We hope you have enjoyed our little play on words.

THE LAY OF THRYM

Thrym was a powerful giant king. His dwelling was deep in Jotunheim, the frosty land of the giants. His castle was large and luxurious, his subjects were many and the quantity and quality of his riches was vast. But he was unhappy. He had everything he wanted except the thing he wanted most of all: a goddess wife. Many a giantess would have been happy and proud to be the wife of such a great giant king, but Thrym, in his travels, had once seen the goddess Freya, Queen of Beauty and Love. Since that time he wanted nothing more than for Freya to come to his kingdom in Jotunheim and be his queen.

The thought of Freya as his wife would not leave him. he could think of nothing else, day and night. His desire built inside him to the point where he decided to risk everything he had, including his life, to have her. He called his giant cousin, Utgard-Loki, who was also a king and the greatest of giant sorcerers, to travel with him to Asgard to carry out his risky plan. Thrym had decided to steal Thor the Thunder God's magic hammer and demand that the only way for the gods to get it back would be by sending Freya to be his wife.

Getting into Asgard would be difficult, stealing Thor's hammer, Mjollnir, would be almost impossible and even if that went well it was not at all certain that Freya would consent to be Thrym's queen. But Thrym was determined to the point of desperation and Utgard-Loki was a great magician. Thrym and Utgard-Loki knew it was a *risk everything* journey and this is how they did it.

Asgard is separated from the other worlds by the Rainbow Bridge which is guarded by Heimdall, the greatest watcher of all time. Heimdall's ears are so good he can hear a bat's wing from across the ocean. His eyes are so good he could see that same bat move an eyelid, at night. And Heimdall never sleeps. The giant kings knew they could not sneak past Heimdall or try to force their way past, so they used magic. Elves come and go across the Rainbow Bridge (and Utgard-Loki used almost all of his magic to disguise himself and Thrym) so Heimdall didn't pay much attention to the two elves who walked by him, even though he didn't know their names. He even snickered a bit and believed their story the next day when they walked out carrying a heavy sack between them. They told him they had sold a magic rope to Loki for a bag of gold.

But in that night the worst thing that could happen, did happen: Thor's hammer was stolen. The gods were gathered in their great feasting hall telling stories of battle and romance to pass the evening. Nobody noticed two elves hiding behind a couch in one lonely corner of the hall. Thor told tales of great battles with giants. Heimdall, who was watching the Rainbow Bridge even as he feasted with the other gods, told of how safe Asgard was because of his watchful eye. The beautiful Sif, wife of Thor, reminded them all of Loki's trickery and the time he had cut off her wondrous golden hair. Loki himself told tales of other treacherous tricks he had played on giants (and sometimes gods) in the past. Freya tried to outdo them all with stories of the many husbands she had had in many lands. Even Odin the Allfather told a tale from before they all were born, for he was among the oldest in all creation.

Thrym and Utgard-Loki waited patiently in their hiding place knowing that the boring stories must soon stop. When they did Thrym quietly snuck through the hall peeking into the sleeping quarters of the gods. He passed the room in which the goddess Freya lay sleeping and stood gazing in wonder at her beauty. He tore himself away and very quietly crept down the hallway to where Thor slept snoring loudly. So determined was Thrym that he was able to take Thor's hammer from right beside his sleeping hand.

You can imagine Thor's anger the next morning. His bellowing filled the hall as he raged about breaking tables and chairs in his search for his lost hammer. No one knew where it was. Nobody had seen anything suspicious. Heimdall assured him that no one had left Asgard carrying his hammer. Yet it was gone and soon all the gods realized what that meant. Without his hammer even Thor would not be able to withstand an attack from the giants if they were to come now. Asgard was in danger.

Only one god was cunning enough to find Thor's lost hammer: Loki. And the only way to search all of the nine worlds would be from the air. So he borrowed Freya's falcon skin and flew away. Far down below in frosty Jotunheim the giants were celebrating Thrym's daring deed. Many had gathered to share in Thrym's triumph. Even the great Fenris Wolf and Jormungand, the Midgard Serpent were there, knowing that the gods were weakened and that plans should be made to attack Asgard.

But Thrym had only one thing on his mind: the Goddess of Love, Freya. He told them of his plan to trade Thor's hammer for Freya's promise to be his wife. It was then that they heard the sound of falcon's wings high, high above them. They knew there were few who would dare to travel to Jotunheim and were quite sure it must be Loki. Loki was sometimes a friend, sometimes an enemy, always one to be listened to and never to be trusted. He was both a god and a giant and they knew he must be the messenger to carry Thrym's wishes back to Asgard. But he didn't need to know that so many powerful giants and friends of giants were gathering so Utgard-Loki wove a powerful spell cloaking all but Thrym from Loki's sight.

Soaring over Jotunheim Loki saw the giant king, Thrym, standing alone on the frozen wastes waving for him to land. Loki glided down and stood beside Thrym with Freya's falcon wings folded on his sides. They exchanged careful greetings, both knowing they needed to quickly get to the point of Loki's visit. Loki began with the tale of Thor's wrath and of the search through all of Asgard for the missing hammer. He was about to continue when Thrym told him he need look no further; the hammer Mjollnir was safely hidden in Jotunheim.

Thrym told Loki his own tale of how he had stolen the hammer (Loki was secretly impressed but tried not to show it) and of how he had hidden it eight miles underground beneath the frozen expanse of Jotunheim. He told Loki how he was willing to risk his life for the greatest prize of all: Freya as his queen. When the gods delivered Freya, they could have the hammer back. Otherwise Thrym would gather a great giant army and storm the walls of Asgard. Loki understood how serious this threat was and promised to deliver Thrym's message to Asgard.

Thor was very happy with the news. Freya in exchange for his hammer seemed like a good trade to him. Freya was furious. Never, never would she marry a giant, even if it meant the fall of Asgard. All tried to change her mind but their arguments grew weaker as her anger flared with each new attempt.

We've heard that Heimdall had excellent vision but it should be known that he could see so well he could even see into the future. What he saw wasn't always as clear as just looking across an ocean. Still, it was a picture of what would probably be and all the gods were surprised as Heimdall suddenly roared with laughter at what he had seen. He told them of seeing the mighty Thor dressed in a wedding gown seated at a banquet in Thrym's feasting hall. They forgot the danger facing Asgard and laughed with Heimdall (all except Thor) knowing that the solution to their problem had been found. They would disguise Thor as Freya and send him to Jotunheim.

Despite Thor's complaints, which he knew were useless, his friends and family dressed him up in the finest satin gown with jewels at his throat, a sash of the finest silk and jingling keys at his waist. Rubies and emeralds adorned his fingers and a bridal veil woven with golden and silver threads covered his face, not to be removed until the wedding ceremony was completed. Loki was to be the bridesmaid and the two climbed into Thor's chariot, drawn by goats, and thundered off to Jotunheim.

What a feast Thrym had prepared! The tables were piled high with food and fresh, clean straw had been spread on all the benches in honour of the special guests. Thrym was beside himself with excitement as he looked across the table at his veiled bride to be. Of course he served her first. Thor was so hungry from the journey that he devoured a whole roast ox, seven giant baked salmon and a platter of bread and then washed it all down with fourteen gallons of beer. Loki looked from guest to guest hoping they wouldn't realize it was Thor in disguise. He was angry and embarrassed but he dare not say anything to make the giants suspicious. Thrym told Loki how amazed he was at Freya's appetite but Loki only answered that she had been so excited about her wedding that she hadn't been able to eat in eight days.

Thrym could control himself no longer. He stood up, leaned across the table and lifted Freya's veil to steal a kiss. Thrym's eyes met the eyes of a Thunder God whose hammer had been stolen and he was so shocked by the glaring, red eyes of Thor that he dropped the veil and sat down without the kiss. Loki had of course seen everything and he had an answer ready for Thrym's next question. He told him that Freya had been looking forward to her wedding night with such uncontrollable excitement that she had not been able to sleep for eight nights. That was why her eyes were so red.

Thrym again jumped to his feet, declared the ceremony finished (Who was going to argue with him?) and raced off to get his "wedding gift" to seal the arrangement. Thor used all his strength to wait until Thrym placed the gift, the hammer Mjollnir, in his lap before he acted. Once his hand closed on Mjollnir's handle, Thor jumped to his feet, ripped off the bridal veil and stood in all his glory as the God of Thunder. With one swift stroke of his hammer Thor cracked Thrym's skull and sent him flying across the hall. All the other giants and guests scattered in fear as Thor stood triumphant with his hammer held high.

CREATION RECITATION

(Two groups of 5 are left and right at the front of the stage area. One group is in blue capes [Niflheim], the other in red capes [Muspellheim]. The remainder of the company is centre stage, near the back. All groups are in tight circles, facing inward. The large, back group is the chorus which recites the following; red and blue are the Eurythmists portraying the creation. All are completely still for the first couplet. With the second, Niflheim begins the movement; with the third couplet, Muspellheim.

Before the dawn of time grew near, there was no sand, no wave.
There were no creatures, gods or men, there was no land, no grave.

Far to the north a mist did rise, a freezing, icy rime,
From frigid rivers raw and bleak in frosty Niflheim

From deepest south where fire reigns with flashing, flaring flame,
A steamy heat did rise and spread from molten Muspellheim.

From Muspellheim to Niflheim, across that endless space,
The searing steam and icy mist towards each other raced.

Although the void was awesome great, Ginnungagap its name,
Cold met with heat in emptiness. Ice burning. Biting flame.

Life quickened in the warming drops that formed where ice met steam.
A giant born of fire and frost, a king without a queen.

His name was Ymir, first to be, and from him sprang his sons
And daughters who did multiply to be the evil ones.

(Ymir is the first to leave the chorus and begin the giants' "camp." When the "ancestor" takes up his position to begin the gods' camp the chorus dissolves and all go to their respective camps. All then take up the recitation and the remaining movement.)

And from the ice that formed that day a giant cow was born.
She fed the giant and licked the ice and there appeared next morn,

The ancestor of all the gods, a hero tall and strong,
Whose children multiplied and spread and thus became a throng.

The giants and the gods soon saw that strife they'd surely give.
And so the worlds nine they formed, that they apart may live.

The giants lived in Jotunheim, a land of frost so cold.
The goddesses and gods did dwell in Asgard's halls of gold.

And though their separate lives they lived, their enmity was deep.
An enmity that flashed and flared and then returned to sleep.

(The two camps face the audience and speak in unison)

THE PANTHEON

We've told aloud from whence we came, in time of distant past.
Let each step forth and speak the name that's kept until the last,
And final days of Ragnarok, the twilight of the gods,
When heroes, giants, demons all are laid beneath the sods.

(Each steps forward to introduce the following in character.)

ODIN: I'm Odin, oldest of the gods, Allfather high and wise.
I'm God of Battle, God of Death, I plucked one of my eyes,
To gain the wisdom of the well, to learn the poetry,
Of ancient runes and magic spells and secret alchemy.

YMIR: I was the first of all that be, a giant of the frost.
My name is Ymir, Odin's foe, I fought with him, and lost.

FRIGGA: To be the queen of Asgard's halls is cause for my own fame.
The mother of the highest gods, and Frigga is my name.

THRYM: I'm Thrym, the king of giant kings, my halls are filled with gold.
My wealth in cattle, jewels, slaves, is stunning to behold.
My power's growing day by day, I lead a kingly life.
I've everything a king could want, except a goddess wife.

THOR: I crash, I smash, the thunder rolls, I'll fight a raging bull.
My hammer breaks through any door, or any giant's skull.
They call me Thor, the Thunder God, the Earth shakes at my name.
The poets tell, the bards do sing my songs of strength and fame.

SIF: I'm Sif, the wife of thundering Thor, my hair was long and gold,
Till Loki snipped it off one night, his heart so icy cold.

LOKI: My shape I change to suit my whim, there's trouble where I stand.
I'm tricky, sly and cunning, too; I spread pain o'er the land.
My friends are few, my foes abound and evil is my game.
I'll catch you if you get too close, and Loki is my name.

HEIMDALL: Let Loki boast, a fool is he, as any here can tell.
He fathers demons, wolves and snakes, he even fathered Hel.
I stand guard at the rainbow bridge, I challenge one and all.
My ears are sharp, my eyes are keen, my name is this: Heimdall.

FENRIR, JORMUNGAND, HEL

ALL 3: We three were fathered by a god, our mother a giant hag.
We call the gods our enemies and of our strength we brag.
F: I'm Fenrir, wolf of monstrous size,
J: I'm Jormungand, the snake. I circle Midgard in the sea,
F & J: For fear the gods do shake.
HEL: I'm Hel, I rule the underworld, the dead sleep in my halls.
ALL 3: The gods we'll fight at Ragnarok, when father Loki calls.

BALDER: They call me good, they call me pure, they call me beautiful.
The goddess Frigga calls me son, to all I'm dutiful.
The birds on Earth sing at my call, the flowers open wide.
I'm known as gentle Balder by the friends close by my side.

UTGARD—

LOKI: My spells of magic charm are strong, a giant king am I.
I'm Utgard-Loki, sorcerer, I stand a mile high.

IDUNA: I keep the precious fruit of life, the apples of acclaim.
To me the gods for youth do come: Iduna is my name.

GERDA: My birthplace was in Jotunheim, inside a giant's hall.
My beauty hypnotized a god, fair Gerda I am called.

FREYR: Indeed her beauty had a power, I gazed from Asgard's heights.
And I, god Freyr, my sword did trade, to win a giant wife.
Oh woe is me, I'll rue the day I gave my magic sword,
When Surt I face, the fiery foe, and and all his fiery hoards.

FREYA: My brother Freyr may think his wife the fairest of the fair.
My beauty shines through all the worlds, the finest jewels I wear.
My name is Freya, Goddess Love, my beauty taunts, cajoles.
I turn the heads of gods and men and even those of trolls.

BROKK,

EITRI: I'm Brokk, I'm Eitri, dwarfs are we, we live in caverns dank.
We forged Thor's mighty hammer true; for it he's us to thank.

TYR: I'm Tyr the brave, I dared to tame the Fenris Wolf so fierce.
I placed my sword hand in his mouth, my bones his teeth did pierce.

ELLI: The strongest men have tried to best me in a wrestling match.
I'm age itself and no one can escape old Elli's grasp.

THE PLAY
THE LAY OF THRYM

SCENE ONE—ASGARD

(All the gods and goddesses are milling around a feasting table. Odin calls imperiously. They obey)

ODIN: Come, gather, my children, my wife and my friends.
With feasting and stories the evening we'll spend.

TYR: Allfather, again how your wisdom you show.
We gods have a history that humans should know.
Let's tell of adventures we've shared in the past,
Of romance and battle by the children thou hast.

FREYR: If stories it be, most of battle and war,
Let's call on the Hurler, the Thundering Thor.

THOR: How right you are, brother. My strength is immense.
My arms are the centre of Asgard's defence.
When whirling my weapon, the winds raging roar,
And giants flee fearful when facing great Thor.

LOKI: Your boasting makes weary, we've heard all we need.
Let Freya, the wondrous, tell now of her deeds.
Her stories of romance in lands far and wide,
Make famous her beauty, (which she does not hide).

THOR: *(to Loki)* Thy tongue shalt thou hold, thou snivelling sneak.
(to Freya) Amuse us with amorous tales, goddess, speak.

FREYA: I've had many husbands, 'tis knowledge that's true.
Some gods, trolls and men and an ogre or two.
But never since ever have I stooped so low,
As to wed a foul giant, so stupid and slow.
My beauty has melted oh many a male heart,
My charms have enchanted, my love arrows dart,
Driving deeply to touch every masculine being.
But never, oh never, some crude giant I'd be seeing!

GERDA: My mother and father were both giants, kind,
But when I met Freyr then I made up my mind,
To live here in Asgard as wife to a god.
Yet still your harsh words in my ears feel so odd.

(Odin is getting upset at the tension brewing at the table. Frigga notices and speaks.)

FRIGGA: As queen of this gathering I ask of you right,
To finish your cups all and bid us good night.
Your words lead to hurting, a thing to avoid,
Especially when Allfather Odin's annoyed.
Tomorrow we'll speak more of deeds of the past,
Of great battles waged and of memories held fast.
But when tempers are edgy, the best thing to do
Is to sleep deep and then start tomorrow anew.

ODIN: Frigga has spoken with words true and wise.
Now off to your chambers to rest weary eyes.

(Most gods exit. Thor and Freya are visible to the audience, sleeping, though far apart. Thrym comes sneaking across the stage and stands gazing enraptured by Freya's beauty. He hatches a plan and steals Thor's hammer, then exits.)

(Thor awakens to find his hammer missing. His anger is monumental: he smashes furniture in his search. The ranting begins.)

THOR: My Mjollnir is missing, my bold hammer gone!
Which dastardly demon, which perilous pawn
Of some sly, lurking power could do such a thing?
When my hands find his throat, then his neck I will wring.
But what if the giants in Jotunheim hear
That my marvellous, wondrous weapon's not near
To my hands which can throw it with such fearful force?
Then they'll crash through the gates of dear Asgard, of course.
Not even the strength of my arms could withstand
All the giants at once if they'd storm through our land.
So find it I must, and not slow and pokey.
But who can I call on to help me? Ah, Loki!

(Loki has been slinking around, unseen by Thor, listening to his musings. He makes his presence known just as Thor's finishing his question about help.)

LOKI: Is that fear that I see in your eyes, brother Thor?
What terrible trouble could cause you to roar
Through our peaceful and beautiful dining saloon,
Smashing tables and chairs like some blundering baboon?

(Thor grabs Loki by the collar and speaks threateningly)

THOR: This is no time for insults, you cowardly cur.
We must find mighty Mjollnir before they're astir. *(he points to the gods)* I could crush your small head just as quick as I'd sneeze,
But I'm asking you kindly to help, brother, please. *(with sarcasm)*

LOKI: Goddess Freya might lend me her falcon skin fine.
Then I'll soar and I'll sail over all worlds nine,
And some clue of your hammer will reach my keen eyes.
For nothing escapes this old master of spies.

(quietly, to Freya who still sleeps)

You must wake, sister dear, we have terrible news.
Brainless Thor here his hammer of power did lose.
I must fly with your falcon skin out of this place,
And come back ere we're smashed by the whole giant race.

FREYA: Your message brings terrible fear to my heart.
If my feathers were silver, I'd bid you depart.
If my feathers were golden, no questions I'd ask.
Put them on, brother Loki, and fly to your task.

SCENE 2—JOTUNHEIM

(As Loki flies over the worlds nine, the scene changes to Jotunheim where Thrym and his subjects are celebrating Thrym's daring scheme. They are singing their battle song and bragging about their superiority over the gods.)

ALL: Jotunheim, Thrym, Jotunheim, Jotunheim!
Jotunheim, Jotunheim, Thrym, Thrym!

THRYM: Oh Jotunheim you land of ice I am your King.
But just what good does all this power to me bring?
On my great throne made all of gold alone I sit.
Oh does my life here make me happy? Not a bit!
O'er endless land so coated with a frosty sheen.
My loneliness is calling for the perfect Queen.
I've seen her slumbering beauty in yon Asgard halls.
I'll risk my life to have her in my palace walls.

(Thrym returns from his reverie and faces his companions.)

THRYM: I've called you all together here today.
To tell you that I've finally found a way,
To force the goddess Freya to my side.
Thor's hammer I did steal and then did hide.

YMIR: What giant woman in our land would not be proud
To be your wife and queen and mother of your brood?
Must Freya be the one you choose to share your life?
The gods we cannot trust. I fear there shall be strife.

BROKK,
EITRI: The hammer that we forged in bygone days?
The hammer filled with magic of our dwarfish ways?
Thor's anger shall indeed be awesome great.
When he finds out then death will surely be our fate.

FENRIR: Without his hammer we have naught of him to fear.
I'll grind his bones between my teeth if he comes near.

JORMUN—

GAND: My coils I shall wrap around his flimsy trunk.
And into Midgard's ocean mighty Thor I'll dunk.

ELLI: Why all this talk of teeth and tails and distant lands?
He'll meet his end if e'er he falls into my hands.

UTGARD—

LOKI: But hark! I hear the sound of beating distant wings.
Who dare approach this gathering of giant kings?
It must be Loki, friend to some and father to a few.
I worry when he's near, and so should you! *(this last bit to the audience)*

THRYM: He must not find us gathered in this giant huddle.
What he reports unto the gods could cause a muddle.
So cloak us, Utgard-Loki with a magic spell,
That me alone he sees so my sly plan goes well.

(With elaborate gestures Utgard-Loki, the master sorcerer, weaves a spell which renders all but Thrym totally invisible.)

UTGARD—

LOKI: We who are here when Loki comes can all see him.
But Loki's eyes shall only see our master, Thrym.

(Loki arrives and finds himself alone [he thinks] with the giant king.)

THRYM: How fares it with the gods and with those puny elves?
Are they still thinking highly of their lowly selves?
What brings you flying here to Jotunheim alone?
Are there not friendly lands in which a tricky god might roam?

LOKI: Things are bad for the elves, things are bad for the gods.
We have turned over mountains and turned over sods.
We have searched every nook and behind every door,
But still we can't find the great hammer of Thor.

THRYM: You might as well give up your futile hammer search.
It's not in any house or hall or barn or church.
It's buried down inside the ground eight miles deep.
And if you find it then of course it's yours to keep.
But I have hid it well and now I bet my life.
The payment for it back will be a goddess wife.
Tell Freya she must come and be my faithful bride.
If she says no we'll storm your walls and crush all those inside.

SCENE 3—ASGARD

(Thrym's laughter accompanies Loki as he flies back to Asgard. The giants exit, Loki joins the gods gathered in council around the feasting table.)

THOR: What news have you brought, brother? Stand straight and tell.
What news of my hammer, or what it befell?

LOKI: Your hammer's not damaged, it's deep underground,
Under Jotunheim's frost, all the giants around.
The mighty King Thrym made a bet with his life.
He will trade back your hammer, for a mere goddess wife.
But he's not easily pleased, not just any will do.
(to Freya) There's only one goddess he wants, Freya, you!

THOR: Then have her he shall and it's not a bad trade.
She shall go to his side. The decision is made.

FREYA: Do you think that a fool such as you runs my life?
I decide on the one who will call me his wife!
Just whose fault is it now that we're all in this mess?
Just whose hammer is lost, bungling Thor? Speak! Confess!

GODS: The question is not one of blame or of fault.
We fear for dear Asgard, from giant assault.
With Loki to Jotunheim you must now fly,
The reason is simple, you know clearly why.

FREYA: No reason you give me will change how I feel.
I don't feel the tiniest giant appeal.
I would rather see Asgard destroyed by great Thrym
Than to spend even one day, YUK!, married to him.

(Heimdall gazes into the future and sees a possible solution. He is very amused as he describes his plan to Thor and the assembled gods.)

HEIMDALL: But surely we gods can come up with a plan
That will trick those dull giants and save our whole clan.
With a veil and a gown and the jewels of a bride,
Those dimwits won't know that it's great Thor inside.

(laughter from the gods, except Thor)

SIF: Ah, Heimdall, your wisdom will save us for sure.
We will dress up my husband in satin, and more.
We will give him a wedding dress down to his knees
And we'll hang from his waist some fine jingling keys.

THOR: You will call me unmanly in woman's attire.
Must I go through such hell, all at Freya's desire?

LOKI: There is no time to argue, a great duty calls
Or by this time tomorrow there'll be giants in these halls.
I'll be your companion, your faithful bridesmaid,
And I'll share in your fate for the tricks that I've played.

(Thor grudgingly consents and the gods begin their gleeful task of bedecking him as befits a bride, sparing no teasing and laughter at his expense.)

FRIGGA: Thou must swallow thy pride, my unfortunate son.
But you'll have the last laugh when this grave chore is done.

IDUNA: We mustn't forget to pin these well-wrought brooches,
To bedazzle the giant when he's looking for smooches.

FREYA: Such a beautiful bridal veil no giant's seen.
All studded with diamonds and emeralds green.
Vulgar Thrym surely finds you a glorious sight,
And can scarce wait the hours till your wedding night.

MALE

GODS: She's gorgeous, she's lovely, oh what is her name?
Does she have a twin sister who looks just the same? *(turning serious)*
We salute you, oh brother, be off to to your fate,
And may fortune smile on you at Jotunheim's gate.

THOR: Bring my goats and my chariot, it's time to depart.
We can get there by evening, if we hastily start.

SCENE 4—JOTUNHEIM

(Thrym and his companions are gathered around a lavishly laid feasting table. Thrym is in his finest kingly clothing and is openly excited about his bride's arrival.)

THRYM: Now everything I've wanted soon will come to be.
The goddess Freya comes tonight to marry me.
We must prepare, these benches look so cold and raw.
They must be padded deep with soft and finest straw.

HEL: The thund'ring hooves of Asgard's goats I hear, unseen.
The time has come to welcome Jotunheim's new queen.

UTGARD—

LOKI: No magic must I use this time to hide each guest.
We sit here waiting each of us so finely dressed.

(Loki and "Freya" arrive. A giant leads the chariot away, they join Thrym.)

THRYM: It's all arranged, the perfect feasting table laid.
(To "Freya") There's food for fifty giants, all so finely made.
        My friends are here to share with me this time of joy.
        Oh, dost thou think that our first child will be a boy?
        But there is time enough when thou and I our hands will hold.
        For thee a seat of honour, ere the food gets cold.

(Thor is feeling very hungry and devours much of what is on the table. Loki is looking around a little worried and embarrassed, the giants are simply amazed.)

THRYM: I simply can't believe the way she drank and ate.
        A whole ox gone and seven salmon on one plate.

LOKI: Since she's known she'd be coming to be your fair mate,
        Not a morsel she's eaten for six days, no, eight!
        So wild with excitement to tell you "I do,"
        She has fasted and saved all her hunger for you.

(Loki's words are enough to arouse desire in Thrym. He leans to Freya and lifts her veil to steal a kiss. He is shocked by her ferocious eyes.)

THRYM: Her eyes are like the burning coals of Muspellheim.
        So fearsome for a goddess fully in her prime.

LOKI: Since she's known she'd be coming to be your fair mate,
        Not a second she's slept now for six nights, no, eight.
        Freya's eyes are ferocious, the red is so deep,
        Her excitement for you, Thrym, has robbed her of sleep.

THRYM: That's *talk* enough of marriage, let the feasting cease!
        Bring out my wedding gift to seal our vows with peace.
        Then Loki you can take the hammer back to Thor.
        And I will live a life with her whom I adore.

(The dwarfs, Brokk and Eitri, carry Thor's hammer with difficulty and place it on Thor's lap. The moment it is in his hand he springs up, tears the bridal veil from his face and crushes Thrym's skull. The others turn tail and flee, calling a fearful version of their battle cry from the song "We Are Giant Warriors." Thor stands triumphant.)

After an appropriate moment, the chaos coalesces into an orderly group of human children facing their audience. The removal of some key piece of costume to signify the transformation from character back to child should be obvious. They are standing facing their parents and peers as themselves, about to deliver the finale.

FINALE

So much of what you've seen today, did happen in true fact.
In days of yore, on some far shore did we great heroes act.
Some battles won, some battles lost, no peace we ever sought,
Returning on the final day of Ragnarok, we fought.

The battle that was waged that day was fought upon the plain,
Where heroes, giants, demons all, were found among the slain.
And o'er the smouldering countryside a dusty wind did blow,
That blew the ashes from the ground, and there new life did grow.

And from the boughs of Yggdrasill, that ever-living tree,
Did two arise, the ancestors of all humanity.
The gods were gone to heavens high, no more did they appear,
To tease or taunt or help or haunt, or at the humans sneer.

So here we stand before you now, grandchildren of that day,
Upon this Earth to live in peace, with your good help, we pray.

Here's a collection of various verses and poems on a wide range of themes.

I AM A HOUSE
A Class Three Housebuilding Poem

I am a house of boards and bricks and glass and steel and stone.
A family within me dwells; I am their hearth, their home.

My fine front door is facing south, my back is to the north.
My left hand greets the rising sun as westward she goes forth.

My walls are strong, my roof is high, I'm rooted in the Earth.
So listen clearly to my words; I'll tell you of my birth.

My roots are concrete buried deep inside the ground below.
To get them there was difficult, laborious and slow.

An excavator dug the trench through grass and soil and sand,
Down to the rock inside the Earth, upon which I now stand.

The forms were built and leveled true, the work of many days.
The fresh cement would surely dry beneath the sun's bright rays.

My footings and foundation then were strong as strong can be.
The carpenters began the work to frame the shape of me.

My walls went up with openings for windows and for doors.
The hammers rapped on ribs of fir, the joists for all my floors.

The hammers banged, the nails sank in and held me all together,
But I was still an open cage, all filled with wind and weather.

The hammers rang, the rafters raised the roof up to the sky.
My ridge was reached and I could see the birds as they flew by.

The hammers tapped their little nails to hold each shake and shingle.
I stood so still but with each tiny tap I'd quake and tingle.

And as each course of shingles made its way up to the top,
The sunlight on my floors below began to dim and stop.

I won't forget the first day that my roof was closed up tight.
My floors stayed dry although it rained and rained that whole first night.

And in the weeks that followed many detailed jobs were done.
The sheathing on my outside walls blocked out the setting sun.

The trades were there in every room to do their varied jobs.
They drilled my studs for pipes and wires, my doors to mount doorknobs.

The plumbers plumbed me high and low, brought water for each need,
To every bath and kitchen sink to wash each dirty deed.

The power people put the proper plugs in perfect places,
To light each room electrically as bright or cozy spaces.

Just so my human occupants are warm or cool all year,
They insulated roof and walls, the weather not to fear.

On every inside wall they covered up with gyproc sheets,
And plastered all the cracks and holes to make it all look neat.

The window people came and then installed each pane of glass.
Now nowhere can the whistling wind through any opening pass.

The final details now were done, the siding and the trim,
The fireplace, the kitchen stove and towels, her and him.

Each doorknob brass and knick-knack glass with loving care is glistening,
But now I must be quiet just in case the family's listening.

VEGETARIAN STEW
(VEGETARIANS, TOO)

Cauliflower white and broccoli green,
In every good garden are sure to be seen.

Red radish you rascal your red is so bright,
But cut you in half and inside you're all white.

New potatoes from the ground
Are sometimes long and sometimes round.

Carrots growing right beside
Are long and orange and sometimes wide.

Parsnip is a long, white root.
When baked it's sweet as any fruit.

Beets are red and round and hard
And grow quite well beside Swiss chard.

Tomatoes are tiny or tennis ball round.
They turn black and slimy if they touch the ground.

Herbs can be spicy and savoury, too,
And can make all the difference 'tween good or bad stew.

Peas in the pod are as cozy as cousins.
In some pods are three and in others are dozens.

Pole beans, lima beans, broad beans, bush beans,
Wax beans, yellow beans, green beans, blue jeans.

My cabbage red and lettuce green and turnips, too, you all may seek,
But leave my little onions, please, and in my garden don't take a leek!

So now my veggie song is done.
Thanks be to Earth and rain and sun.

FRACTION ACTION POEMS

For A Group Of Eight

Together as a whole we're one,
Our strength is firm and true.
Divide us down the middle and
In halves we stand as two.

A half in half becomes a fourth,
Or quarter, as you know.
It's funny as the groups grow small,
Their number seems to grow.

Now halve a quarter yet again,
Our parts are scattered wide.
A fractioned whole, we're each an eighth.
No more can we divide.

For A Group Of Nine

We are one, we are whole, we are we.
We can split, not in half, but in three.
We're a third, we're a third, so are we.

Add a third to a third and you'll see,
That two-thirds are what we now must be.
Add the third third WE'RE WHOLE, you'll agree.

Let's divide one more time into three.
Split each three into three and you'll see,
How we ninths are pure geometry.

For A Group Of Twelve

Wealthy Twelve

Twelve is a number that is rich as any wealthy King.
Cut it down the middle and you still can do 'most anything.
One six can split in half and form two lovely sets of three,
The other breaks up into pairs to dance a reel so gleefully.
Couplets, triplets back to sixes, circle round for one whole twelve.
The magic of division helps us as we into fractions delve.

Twelve is a number that can break up into many parts.
Fours are there as square as square like dots on dice or wheels on carts.
Each of those three fours, of course, can use the fraction name one third,
And each can give a member to create a new group with the word
One quarter as its fraction name and now we've reached the very end.
Please don't divide a twelve by five or broken hearts you'll have to mend.

Ten

What can you do with a ten?
Cut in half for two fives but what then?
You can try but you can't cut again.
Let's go back to the whole and divide,
Into twos nicely placed side by side.
Back to ten, two by five, multiplied.

Two's a Pair

One, two, buckle my shoe, not much else here we can do.
We can walk along together, or break apart in stormy weather.

SIX

6 is always 1 X 6, whether chestnuts, rocks or sticks.
6 together in a pile, count them carefully, and smile.

12 is always double 6, make 2 piles, each has 6.
2 X 6 or 6 X 2, 12 is what they'll always do.

18's always triple 6. Nice and neat! Don't let them mix!
3 good piles all the same. 6 in each. 18's the name.

24 spread on the floor, make nice piles, there'll be 4.
6 per pile, never more, 4 X 6 is 24.

30 things in groups of 6, 5 new piles, there's no tricks.
Like the fingers on one hand, 5 X 6 in every land.

36 is 6 X 6, make 6 piles, each has 6.
6 X 6 is 36, I'm tired of the number 6.

42 came down from heaven, 6 per pile times number 7.
7 X 6 is 42. Yabba dabba dabba doo.

48 is quite a few. 8 X 6 is what you do.
8 new piles, each has 6. 6 X 8 or 8 X 6.

54 is even more. 9 new piles on your floor.
54 is 9 X 6, yes 54 is 9 X 6.

60 ending with a zero. 10 X 6 with 10 the hero.
Multiplying 6 by 10 will give us 60. Now! and then!

66 the magic number. 11 X 6, now don't you slumber!
Double digit 66. It's 11 X 6 for clickety-clicks.

72's as far as we go. 12 X 6, why, don't you know?
Yes 12 X 6 is 72. I'm 6 feet tall; how about you?

SEVEN

7 in a group by itself.
1 little pile on the shelf.

14 is 2 times that 7.
14 is double one 7.

21, 21, you're 7 X 3.
3 piles of 7, 21 you'll be.

28, 28, you're 7 X 4.
7 X 4, 28 and no more.

35, oh 35, you're 5 X 7 or 7 X 5.
Multiply an ODD by 5, the answer always ends with 5.

42, oh 42, you're 6 x 7, you 42.
6 X 7 is 42. Yabba dabba dabba doo.

49 is 7 X 7.
Magic numbers squared in heaven.

56 in piles of 7.
8 big piles, each has 7.

63, the piles count 9.
7 in each. Yes, every time.

70 total, 10 X 7.
10 X 7. Pigs in heaven.

77's 11 X 7.
11 X 7 is 77.

84 does 12 adore.
12 X 7 is 84.

A PRETTY LOUSY POEM

Itch, scratch, itch, scratch.
Behind my ear I have a batch,
As big as Grandma's cabbage patch,
Of crawling, biting, nasty lice
That multiply as fast as mice.

Itch, scratch, itch, scratch.
The nits are just about to hatch,
And then I'll have another batch,
As big as Grandma's cabbage patch,
Of crawling, biting, nasty lice
That multiply as fast as mice.

I've shampooed once, I've shampooed twice.
Believe me please, it's not so nice,
To find behind my other ear,
So close that I can almost hear,
A brand new crawling, nasty batch,
That make me itch and make me scratch,
With nits that soon will want to hatch,
And turn into another batch of
AAAAAAAARRRRRRRRRGGGGGGGG.

AN HOUR LONG POEM

Tick, tock, goes the clock, counting seconds one by one.
Round and round the thin hand goes, it never speeds, it never slows.
Sixty seconds each time 'round,
Tick, tock, tick, tock's the only sound.

Tick, tock, goes the clock, counting minutes one by one.
I watch the minute hand as well as anybody here can tell,
But somehow I don't see it budge, it surely travels slow as sludge.
Yet there it is, it's at the line, another minute past in time.

Tick, tock, goes the clock, counting minutes five by five.
The numbers on the face look just the same as any other place.
But with them sure as bees make hives,
To count along I must use fives.

One is five and two is ten and I must learn to count again.
Fifteen minutes, says the three, it's quarter past, oh now I see.
Four's not four, it's twenty now and I am understanding how.
Five times five is twenty-five and to the bottom I'll soon dive.

The minute hand is at the six and this is one of many tricks
We learn to tell the time of day, that six is thirty, yea oh yea!
Seven times five is thirty-five, then why do we say twenty-five
To five or six or ten or three? We're climbing up, oh now I see.

To go by fives is oh so fast, and like the three says quarter past
At nine it's quarter to, at last.
Fifteen more until the top, when we get there will all time stop?
The number ten has special power: it says its name, ten to the hour.

Ten and nine and eight and seven, it's six, it's five to at the eleven.
Now four, now three, now two, now one, we're almost there, we're almost done.
The second hand in all its haste, now sixty times around has raced.
We're at the twelve, the clock says BONG, oh sixty minutes was so long.

Tick, tock, goes the clock, counting seconds one by one.
Round and round the thin hand goes, it never speeds, it never slows.
Sixty seconds each time 'round, tick, tock, tick, tock's the only sound.
Tick, tock, tick, tock, tick, tock, tick, tock, tick, tock, tick, tock . . . .

I AM A STONE

I am stone so hard and round,
I sit so still, I make no sound.
I am so big, a mountain's shoulder,
No tiny pebble, I am a boulder.
An earthquake rumbles, the mountains shake,
And heavy pieces crack and break.
They slip and slide and roll and drop,
In lush green valley, they land and stop.

THE LIFE OF ST. MARTIN

helper of the poor and needy

Many centuries back into history,
Long before all our elders were born,
In a time that is shrouded in mystery,
In a land that was ravaged and torn
By the wars of the great Roman Empire,
Lived a boy and his mother alone,
In a village beside a calm river,
In a cabin of wood and of stone.

The young boy, age of six, was named Martin,
How his mother was called, we don't know.
He stayed home, didn't have kindergarten,
But his hands knew the spade and the hoe.
With his mother he learned of the flowers,
From the stories she told by his side,
As they worked in their garden for hours,
Near the river so deep and so wide.

In the evenings she'd sing of her people,
All the songs that her mother had sung.
Till the village bell rang from the steeple,
And their heads, work a'weary, were hung.
They would laugh, they would cry, they would cuddle,
They would share every sorrow and joy.
Till one day something new brought a muddle,
To the lives of this mother and boy.

This new thing that did stir and did bother,
All the peace of the life that they led,
Was the sudden return of his father,
Roman soldier they thought to be dead.
To the Caesar he'd been a good servant,
Making war in some far distant land.
To his loyalty always observant,
Many enemies died at his hand.

Now in those days, in that distant country,
What the father commanded was law.
He removed his son Martin from family,
So the life of a soldier he saw.
He must be Romanized, came the order,
Martinus was the name he now bore.
In a camp near the Gallian border,
Now began his hard training for war.

Martinus, still a young boy of seven,
Had to serve in the kitchen so hot,
Till his memories of his young heaven,
Disappeared, and the songs he forgot.
Three long years, chopping wood, hauling water,
Like a slave in the kitchen he'd work.
So exhausted that sometimes he'd totter,
And with beatings he'd wake with a jerk.

But his feelings grew hard as he hurried,
From each strenuous task to the next.
And his masters were no longer worried,
As they saw how his strong muscles flexed.
It is time that he went to the stables,
To the ways of the soldier he'll turn.
Long enough has he served at the tables,
Now the ways of the horse he will learn.

Three more years Martinus did hard labour,
Now his master a kind stable groom,
Hauling hay for each horse and its neighbour,
Growing callous from shovel and broom.
Every saddle and rein, every bridle,
Every hoof, mane and wither he knew.
Long he worked, every day, never idle,
As his love for the animals grew.

As a groom there were none who were better,
As a rider he learned every trick.
For a week he could ride, any weather,
Even hungry or tired or sick.
All his masters were pleased with his learning,
He could ride with the best in the land,
For the life of the soldier he's yearning,
Now to weapons he must turn his hand.

All the years of hard work now seemed easy,
When his training with weapons began.
Hauling water and wood were so breezy,
Now he must build the strength of a man.
From the soldiers he learned all the weapons,
From the sword to the club to the lance.
On the battlefield, anything happens,
There is nothing to leave up to chance.

Two long years Martinus did hard training,
Whether horseback, on foot or at night.
Whether sunny or snowing or raining,
He was trained to be brave and to fight.
Now the emperor called him to battle,
He must travel to some distant land.
With a thousand young men in the saddle,
He must charge with his sword in his hand.

They were fearsome and proud, they were Roman.
He was strong, he was brave, he was armed.
Every horseman and footman and bowman,
Knew that they could be killed or be harmed.
Then they rushed with their horses beneath them,
And they clashed with the enemy fierce.
All around lay the dead and the wounded,
When a spear Martin's helmet did pierce.

Martin fell from his place in the saddle,
With the blood running free from his wound.
As the snow quiet fell on the battle,
He grew weaker, and weaker and swooned.
Soon the great Roman army was winning,
And the enemy soldiers all fled.
On command they gave chase on their horses,
Leaving Martinus lain with the dead.

Two long days did he lie on the war field,
On his winter cloak frost from his breath.
With the snow piling high on his war shield,
While his spirit did battle with death.
In his dreams he saw pictures of mother,
That awoke from his boyhood, his source.
Then his ear felt the breath of another,
And his cheek felt the lips of his horse.

Two long days he had lain with the fallen,
But his horse had returned to its man.
And it felt still the lifespark within him,
And beside him for two days did stand.
Now he rose on his legs weak and shaking,
Cleaned and bandaged the gash on his head.
Kind young Martin, the singer, awaking,
And the crude Roman, Martinus, dead.

Many weeks with his horse did he wander,
And he sang every song that he knew.
And his heart filled with joy as he'd ponder,
In the future the good things he'd do.
All the stories he'd heard as a child,
Were alive in his heart as he rode.
When he thought of his mother he smiled,
And her memory warm in him glowed.

Can I ride along this road forever?
No! The world needs the work of my hands.
There is one thing I know, that I'll never
Ride as soldier to conquer strange lands.
But what task in my future lies yonder?
In what service can I use my strength?
Must I aimless and pointlessly wander
Through the countryside's full breadth and length?

And in that very moment of seeking,
What his life's work before him must be,
He then heard a frail voice to him speaking,
And it clearly did say "please help me."
There beside him right near a small river,
Lay a man stiff and trembling with cold.
With each breath he would quake and he'd quiver,
He was sick, he was weak, he was old.

Martin felt a brisk wind come a'breezing,
And it carried the winter's full force.
Here before him a poor man lay freezing,
While he sat warmed from greatcloak and horse.
Then at once came the end to life's riddle,
Now he knew his task till he grew older.
And he slashed his cloak right down the middle,
And wrapped one half around the man's shoulders.

Disbelief was his only expression
For the man had expected to die.
Where before there had been deep depression,
Now pure gratitude streamed from his eyes.
Martin brought the old man to a city,
Took a room in a warm, cozy inn.
Heard his story with deep, heartfelt pity,
And for both a new life did begin.

In that night Martin had a clear vision.
In his dream he was told by Christ's voice,
That by helping he'd made a decision,
And that now he was faced with a choice.
As a soldier you promised your service,
With each person you help, you serve me.
When you serve even one needy person,
You are serving all humanity.

Martin saw how the townsfolk's hearts hardened,
How the sick and the poor were cast out,
So he bought a small house with a garden,
And he gathered the poor thereabout.
Martin tended the sick and the needy,
With the able he worked in the soil.
All worked hard, did their best, none were greedy,
And together they sang as they toiled.

So you see, all you people before us,
How the spirit of Martin lives on.
Listen well, mark our words, hear this chorus.
Each new moment we live's a new dawn.
We the stronger can all help the weaker,
As the tale of St. Martin has shown.
We are strengthened each time we get meeker,
And we see that our cloak's not our own.

THE WOODLATHE

Buttress bowl and bottle burl,
Birch and alder, maple twirl.
Ash and locust, yew and elm,
Remnants of the forest realm.

Lathe and chuck and finest steel,
Turning true on even keel.
Objets d'art or just doodadding,
Functional and value adding.

VERSE FOR CROSS-STITCH

With my left hand I reach to the Star of the North
And I open my palm and I call its power forth.
And I grasp it and clasp it for all I am worth
And I bow and I bind with the power of the Earth.

With my right hand I reach to the Milky Way bright,
And I gather the power of its heavenly light.
And I feel as it courses through hand, heart and foot,
And I bow to the Earth, there the power to put.

Now I stand straight and tall, the human I be,
With my hand and my gaze reaching eternity.
Into darkness behind me I reach and I hold,
Gaining strength from the past and my ancestors bold.

To the north and the south like a cross now I reach,
And I open my mind while their wisdom they teach.
Now the power of the Earth I will bring to my heart,
As I treasure these gifts, now my work I may start.

designed to be spoken facing east (in the northern hemisphere)

Some accompanying thoughts to VERSE FOR CROSS-STITCH

I wrote this verse at the request of the handwork teacher of the Nelson Waldorf School. She wanted something which not only stated the idea of crosses in verse form, but also embodied the concept through movement in different directions. Accordingly, I wrote the verse standing up, feeling each cross as it coursed through my own body. After quickly jotting a line I returned to my position and allowed the next cross to pass through me. This verse was truly born of movement; I was simply the vehicle to get the words onto paper.

The verse should be spoken and acted facing east (in the northern hemisphere) to accommodate the actions. It begins in a wide spread stance by grasping the power of the North Star, bending at the waist and placing it on, or in front of, the right foot. The second verse repeats the motion from right to left. In the third stanza the children are standing with feet together, the open left hand stretched forward palm down, the arm parallel to the floor. The cross is created when the children carefully reach behind them (if I can do it, they can) until their right arm is in line with the left and also parallel to the floor, a closed fist palm down. For the first two lines of stanza four the children are standing with arms outstretched, left and right. Their hands are palm up, accepting the gifts offered. With line three they bring their arms to cross over their chests, right over left and complete the verse thus.

ON TURNING FIFTY

If seven is magic, then what of its square?
It's magic times magic and you've just been there!
Full forty-nine years as a being of Earth,
Since your eyes saw the light on the day of your birth.

It's a number that carries profundities deep,
When a spiritual wisdom emerges from sleep.
When the teacher within you is ripe and mature
And as mentor of power you're standing so sure.

Full forty-nine years, an accomplishment bold,
To your peers and your juniors a sight to behold.
Now it's come to an end, it's over, it's done.
What you now have is magic times magic, plus one!

BIRTHDAY VERSES

These short verses are designed to be memorized and recited by an individual. Find the one or ones which suit you or a child in your life and let its recitation become a meditation.

In the circle of the ocean wide where sky and water greet,
A lonely island, naught but rock, perhaps you'll some day meet.
That rock has strong and sturdy stood, its only friend the waves
Which crash so mighty on its walls, there are no homes, no graves.
Yet sure as time creeps steady on, the waves unleash their power.
They scratch and wear and etch and grind, each second, minute, hour.
In one soft spot the island can't defend against the wave.
The pebbles, sand and nuggets fall and soon there is a cave.
That cave is now an ancient den where magic makes its lair,
The treasure that's inside is peaceful, gentle, loving, fair.

The sounds seems larger than the hut from which it streams.
The evening air brings forth the tones like gentle dreams.
At times it sounds like falling rain on thirsty grass,
Then bellows with the sound of deep and booming brass.
The harpist's hands fly swiftly o'er the many strings.
Her nimble fingers make us think that now an angel sings.
Oh such a song in praise of forest, ocean, beast
A song of God's creation for the greatest and the least.

A light from the depths of the ocean, can shine like a brilliant star.
The sand holds a creature so humble, yet divers will travel so far
To seek for the treasure that's waiting, inside of that oyster's coarse shell,
The light of the world revealing the beauty that holds like a spell.
That pearl of infinite splendour that shines with a heavenly sheen,
Will find its new home ringed with diamonds atop the great crown of a queen.
She'll wear it on her royal journey, she'll travel to lands near and far,
The light from the depths of the ocean, will shine like a brilliant star.

I'll tell you how I build a house, my secret I will share.
The finest tools I will use, my level, plumb and square.
For generations I will build, the secret's in the ground,
I'll dig to bedrock so my house will sit so safe and sound.
I'll measure with my straightest rule, each room will be so grand,
I'll pour a strong foundation base on which my house will stand.
Each brick and board will be the best, each task of greatest worth.
My dwelling's head will stroke the sky, its feet will grip the Earth.

In a land so far from here, on a sea that's rocked by gentle waves,
To the shore a boat comes near, from the shore a fisher friendly waves.
In the boat the people watch, as the wind and wave caress the shore.
From the land the net is tossed, and the fisher catches many more.
With the water to her knees, her net she casts into the brine.
Her whole life is in these seas, tonight her friends will kingly dine.
As the sun sinks in the west, a final, mighty, awesome throw.
With her full net in her arms, back to the shore she turns to go.

The flight of a dove like an angel can seem.
His moves are so graceful like magic or dream
As he soars high above over forest and field,
At evening a heavenly power he'll wield.
For when the sky darkens all painted with red,
His words are so simple, so easily said,
He'll sing to the people he watched from above.
A message of harmony, true peace and love.

I feel inside my hidden heart, a gurgling, bubbling spring.
Its magic waters soothe the soul and heal 'most everything.
It quenches thirst and fills with life the driest of the dry.
It's like a spark of magic flame beneath the blackest sky.
And when the world's magic gets all hidden from my soul,
The compass of my heart will draw me to the true North Pole.
And if I seek for wisdom to my left or to my right,
The needle always points inside, to my own inner light.

I've lain on my belly and pondered the bugs and the moss and the grass.
They showed me the kingdoms of gnomes and of fairies through their looking glass.
I've flown with the albatross, glided with eagles with eyes in their heart.
The world lay below like a tapestry woven by masters of every fine art.
The eye in my heart sees the beauty in forest and ocean and beast.
My mind sees the goodness in nature's creations, the greatest, the least.
I'll fly with that eagle while keeping my toes gripping firmly the ground.
I'll listen to silence and hear all the glory of purest celestial sound.

The blacksmith grips his tongs, again the iron is thrust to heat.
With steady arm he strikes, his blows an awesome rhythmic beat.
The forge's fire flares, a thousand firefly sparks rain down.
The heavy hammer falls, the clang is heard throughout the town.
His eye, his hand, his will, the craftsman shapes the stubborn steel.
He forges every tool, a horseshoe, nail or wagon wheel.
The anvil takes the blow, and helps the master to the end.
They shape each item true, it will not break and never bend.

Inside a ray of light I stand,
In sunshine pure, in goodness grand.
To every person, plant and beast,
The light brings beauty, truth and peace.
I lift my head and face the sun,
And feel that we are joined as one.
Upon the Earth I stand so still
And turn pure light into pure will.

From riverbank grey comes the heavy dark clay,
With water the potter kneads briskly.
This formless grey mass starts to take on real class
As it spins on the potter's wheel swiftly.
The potter's quick feet turn the wheel true and neat
As his hands do a dance oh so clever.
With the skill of his will he can form mug or jug;
Will the water leak out, surely never.
The force of the flames in the kiln's roaring fire
Turns the clay of the pitcher to stone.
The potter is pleased how his craft serves his needs
And the powers of the Earth serve his home.

Afloat on waters vast and black a tiny ship seeks harbour's peace.
With upright back the sailor's gaze into the night will never cease.
The moon shines down among the stars to light the waves and ocean swells.
The sea air sweeps across his face and brings his nose the ocean smells.
And though that distant land is not yet seen the sailor trusts the sky.
He knows the stars and moon will guide his path and lead him on
To safer shores and there with joy he'll sing and cry.

Near mountain peaks a thousand trickles gather into one.
They form a torrent rushing in the heat of melting sun.
And from the mountain's heights the water carves its own true tracks.
It carries rocks which smash the cliffs and gushes out through cracks.
Now at the edge the river plunges down the mountain face.
The waterfall then splashes in a pool, a quiet place.
And further out that pool reflects the starlight from above,
The twinkling sends to us below the gift of heavenly love.

A journey of gathering begins in the heights where the land meets the sky.
A spring trickles free and begins its descent over rock, ice and snow.
It soaks up the sunshine, the strength of the Earth, as the ground rushes by.
It's blessed by the plants, by the air, by the colours, through which it must flow.
It opens its arms to accept every gift as it glides to its goal.
It passes through richness receiving its share with no asking or greed.
It reaches the shore and brings all of its gifts to the great ocean soul.
It is one with the waves and the deep, it has finally done its great deed.

With the dew of the night still wet on the grass
The shepherd goes out with her flock.
The dawn is still breaking, soon sunrise will pass,
She leads them, a steady, slow walk.
The grass on the pasture is deep, fresh and green,
The sun is now high in the sky.
The flocks feeds in peace, no danger is seen,
They're safe under her watchful eye.
By evening the sun settles low in the west,
And sinks slowly into the sea.
The shepherd removes a small flute from her vest,
They go home in sweet melody.

There's magic in the bushes, there's magic in the leaves,
There's magic in the stems and twigs, kissed by a gentle breeze.
Off in a distant corner, this magic plant does grow.
Its leaves each guard a precious gem, with inner light aglow.
Its rubies, opals, emeralds, its diamonds, sapphires, jade,
And shiny black obsidian, wait in the leaves' cool shade.
These stones and many others, all carry from the Earth,
The blessed goodness of the force that forged them at their birth.
And when the sun shines brightly, on one and every gem,
They'll radiate the love and peace, that lives in each of them.

The trusting seed has sprouted,
The wheat is growing tall.
The stalks wave gently in the wind,
Their strength is felt by all.
Alone they stand so thin and bending,
Each could fall to ground.
Together strong through any storm
They sing a joyous sound.

The tall tree is full of the forest delight.
It guides through the day and it shelters by night.
The apple tree reaches to left, right and up,
Gives shade to the traveller and sweetness to sup.
Some days I'm a tall tree and some days a wide,
With always my roots in the ground deep inside.

Rose red, rose yellow, rose pink, rose white,
You shine as if with inward light.
The sun glows down to warm your face,
Reflecting off all who share your space.
Each rose on the bush reflects the same sun,
Together a glorious bouquet you've become.

The colours of the rainbow seven,
Bathe the world with light from heaven.
I feel the red, the blue, the green
Shine down on me with lustrous sheen.
And as I walk along my friend-filled way,
That light shines out from me and
Joins the awesome light of day.

The skipping stone has a strong big brother.
His father a cliff,
A mountain, his mother.
Brother rock holds the wall of that house on the ridge.
He's the keystone supporting that great river bridge.
Ah, how our feet feel safe with brother beneath us.

The beauty of the pearl
Can be seen in all around us.
The garden flowers soothe our eyes,
The lilac trees astound us.
Each pebble is a priceless gem,
Each cherry, leaf or mouse.
I savour what each new day shows.
The whole world is my house.

The northern lights weave magic in the sky.
Our human hands weave magic when they try.
With wool the colours of the rainbow's glow,
We shape and shape and then create,
A picture full of life and love
That shines out with a beauty that will match
The best of any garden's flowery show.

The fire, the rain, the air, the land,
The farmer holds within her hand,
To shape and knead and bend and take,
To wisely use but never break.
She knows too much of one will harm,
The precious life upon her farm,
And so she learns each proper measure,
Creating now a growing treasure.

The butterfly watches the ducks in the pond.
She whispers a message in one duckling's ear.
She waves with her wings such a soft magic wand.
The duckling looks up with a smile. Did she hear?
Paddle duckling, paddle strong.
Paddle with your duckling brothers.
Paddle hard but paddle calm.
Strength you'll find beside the others.

Apple tree, pear tree, peach tree and plum.
In your cool shade when day is done,
The farmer work a'weary rests.
You give him strength with your sweet fruit.
He feels your strength in leaf and root,
Upon your bark his back is pressed.
Into the Earth your grip is strong.
Your blossoms sweet, your branches long,
For every weather you are dressed.

From grass ground to fence post the quick squirrel races,
Behind him the loyal, alert old dog chases,
Protecting the farm of his master.
The nibbling deer and the prowling skunk,
Coyote and fox and even great bear,
All run from the barking and bristling hair
Of the loyal old hound as he stands his firm ground,
Protecting the farm of the master.

The Prince riding out on his steed of pure white,
Looks out on his land to his left and his right,
He knows that his horse carries him all around
And without him he'd stand small and slow on the ground.
Oh steed serve your master, he knows where to go.
You give him his power, to you he will show
That he knows horse and rider are joined to the end,
And that master and servant call each other, friend.

Caterpillar, butterfly, kitten and cat.
Live in the hayloft above the old barn.
Careful little mouse, you'll get caught just like that.
Kitty is working, you see, it's her farm.
Kitty remember you share this sweet home.
Cows down below you, the goats by the wood.
Horses are out in the field where you roam.
Don't scratch the hand as it brings you your food.

There is a little cowbird, sits on the ox's back.
He likes the way the ox moves slowly,
Steady down the plowing track.
The ox allows the bird to stay and pick each flea and fly.
Together in the field they live
And to each other comfort give
As each day warm or stormy passes by.

Firefly flying over field, farm and town.
Your dream is to fly till you see way, way down
On the people and cities and mountains and trees.
You have flown to the sky, you shine out on the seas.
Now your light is enormous, you shine like the moon.
You can make a sharp shadow of grizzly or loon.
In the night people walk by the light that you throw.
You will soon be the sun, just continue to grow.

The whispering wind has caught your ear,
The sun has caught your eye.
But you still see the candle's spark,
You hear a kitten sigh.
Oh owl trust your wisdom,
Even when your back is turned.
Your friends know they can count on you,
Their friendship you have earned.

Sun follows rain follows wind follows hail.
Spring melts the winter, throws open the jail
Of the life trapped in ice till the summer is here
And the fall follows fast and makes winter draw near.
Over and over the circle goes round.
I reach to the sky with my feet on the ground.
I grow with each season as it passes by.
I'm a beast on the ground I'm a bird in the sky.

A shining star among his brothers,
Sheds his light to show the others,
Where their paths will lead them.
In the forest, silent, listening.
Two deer stand with eyes a'glistening,
Near the path that leads them.
See the child boldly trying,
With his own strength he's relying
On the path that leads him.

The pony raced across the open, grassy, rolling plain.
He heard a boy by forest's edge call out his secret name.
He turned and slowly walked toward this shining magic game.
To one who watched across that vast and broad expanse,
This game looked like a laughing, spinning, limbs a'flying dance.
Who carried whom as o'er the plain they shared a name
And there with hoof and hand and foot did prance.

How could the berry bush without the sparrow grow?
She scatters seeds which fall upon the ground below.
She eats so few, it makes no mark, the others still can feed.
The bush has fruit enough to fill a hungry need.
And when the branches dry are hanging in the autumn air,
New life is waiting for the future berries there to share.

The sprouting young seed gave its trust to the air,
To the sun, to the rain, to the farmers who care.
Will it be a sunflower or a pole climbing bean,
A turnip, a pumpkin, or a cucumber green?
I know for a fact, I can tell you indeed.
The secret most surely is locked in the seed.

She helps her little goslings
As they float about the pond.
She shows them where the finest
Floating food can best be found.
She dives beneath the water
And she shows them where to look.
She teaches them to be so safe
On pond and land and brook.

A lone yellow dandelion grew in the grass.
She tried hard to grow up tall but knew they would pass.
The green rose around her as she stood in their shade.
The grass up now above her head, each stalk and each blade.
She reached down into the Earth and found there her power.
She tried hard with all her might and became a sunflower.

A songbird woke and listened to her cousins sweetly sing.
I slept, she thought, but how I love their voices' golden ring.
I'll listen as they sing their ever joyful song,
And then the melody I'll know and I can sing along.
And so it was with tiny notes that she did start,
And now she sings her cousins' songs with all her heart.

A flock of lambs pranced out across the pasture green.
Their mothers looked to where the little ones had last been seen.
They bleated warnings calling to their young behind the hill.
Their voices carried through the air so calm and still.
The lambs knew nothing of the fox or wolf or bear.
They felt the trust, they knew they must,
Return and from the old ones wisdom learn and share.

A heavy harvest is now done, the farmer sees his golden wheat,
Which flourished in the summer sun and ripened in the August heat.
The miller carries with his hands, the kernels fine, the golden grain,
The bounty from the farmer's lands, the sun, the wind, the Earth, the rain.
The stones are turning in the mill, the river gifts its mighty power.
The wheat is crushed through human will, transformed into a silken flour.
The baker measures, mixes, kneads. Her dough is salty, sweet or mild.
The loaves will quench all human needs, there's bread for every hungry child.

The wind whispers secrets of a place far away,
Full of valleys and meadows and fields of sweet hay.
Bright flowers of red, gold and yellow and blue,
Seem to radiate sunshine with each glowing hue.
And strong as a mountain in midst of those flowers,
A tree straight and tall grows with natural powers.
His roots reach past boulders so deep in the ground
His tip to the sun, all his branches surround.
Beneath him the ground is in soft cooling shade,
For people and beasts a fine shelter he's made.

I look across and see the path on which I tread continue onward.
The bridge before me seems so small I'm filled with dread, I must go forward.
The river rages far below its churning waters sing so sweetly
I think of all the other children, sons and daughters, who there might greet me.
The wind is howling all around, now east now west, the bridge is shaking.
Just room for one, I have no guide in this dark test, my legs are quaking.
Behind a tree a child's hand on yonder shore is to me waving.
Who calls me there from hidden spot, I must know more, my life be saving.
A heavy load is on my back, its weight is great, my strength is fading.
I can't turn back, the path is blocked, I'll face my fate, my future's waiting.

I take a step onto the bridge, the wood is slick, I must go forward.
I look across and see the path on which I tread continue onward.
That child's hand is calling me, it's urging on, despite the danger.
Who will it be, who greets me there on yonder shore, a friend or stranger?
I gaze ahead, not right nor left, not up nor down, the far bank nearing.
The stranger waits to take my hand, I see it's me, I'm through my fearing.

CLOSING VERSE

Our work is done, our day is past,
We'll go our separate ways.
And I will hold so tight and fast
What I have learned today.

I've given with my heart and mind
The effort that it needs.
And I will strive in me to find,
Good thoughts, good words, good deeds.

Here's a collection of retold fables for reading or telling followed by distillations into verse form for recitation.

THE MISER AND HER GOLD

There was once a rich old woman who nobody knew was rich. This was because she wore old clothes, lived in a small, old house and was rarely seen spending any money. All of her riches were hidden in one bag of gold coins which she kept buried in her back yard where no prying eyes could see.

Like most misers, she hated to spend any of her money, but she loved to see it and feel it and most of all, count it. Every day (sometimes twice) she would sneak into her back yard, look behind every bush and tree to make sure nobody was watching, then dig up her sack of gold. She would carefully pour the gold out onto an old (of course) blanket and make piles of big gold coins, piles of medium size gold coins and piles of small gold coins. She counted each size, she counted each pile, she added them all up in her head then just sat for a while looking at them. Sometimes she would hold a big gold coin in one hand and a little gold coin in the other hand and feel which was heavier. She liked the little coins, but she loved the big ones.

On special days the old miser even spread them all out and looked at each one, front and back, until she knew them all so well that if even one were ever to go missing, she'd know right away. On very special days she would lie on her back on the blanket, pile the coins on herself and then close her eyes and pretend that she was buried in gold.

Now there came a day when the miser was being a little too loud while she was playing with her coins. Every true thief knows the sound of jingling coins and on this sunny autumn afternoon a thief was passing by behind the garden wall. That sounds like a lot of coins and of all different sizes, thought the thief, so he stopped and stood silently behind the wall. The old woman was so wrapped up in her counting that he even risked moving carefully along the wall until he found a spot where he could just barely see what she was doing without being seen himself. Surely she'll soon take her treasure back inside, he thought.

To his surprise he watched as she put the bag into a hole in the ground, filled the hole with dirt and carefully spread the spot with dry leaves from a nearby tree so nobody could tell that there had ever even been a hole. He watched the old miser go into the house. He watched the sun go down and he watched it get dark. He saw the miser eat a miserly supper by the light of a candle stub. She was barely finished when she blew out the candle and disappeared into another room, probably to bed.

The thief was very patient. He waited and he watched and saw no light from the house. When he thought it must be the middle of the night, he climbed silently over the wall, brushed away the leaves and removed the soft earth from the hole with the bag of gold coins. He was not only a patient, daring and cunning thief, he was also a mischievous thief. After he had removed the bag he very carefully filled in the hole and covered it again with leaves before climbing quietly over the wall and disappearing into the night.

In the morning the old miser glanced out the window to make sure her treasure had not been disturbed. She decided to wait until the warmer sun of the afternoon before digging up her treasure and spent the day busying herself with miserly things.

Imagine her horror when she discovered her precious treasure had been stolen. She started crying quietly to herself but that wasn't enough. She wept out loud with tears dripping onto her lap, but even that wasn't enough. So she screamed and wailed with the loudest voice she had. Before long her nearest neighbour was standing beside her patting her on the back and asking what was wrong.

She told him the whole story of her bag of gold and how she dug it up every day. The miser's neighbour could not believe that she had been rich. He looked at her clothes and at her house and asked her why she never used any of her riches to buy clothes with no holes in them or to fix her shabby old house. She only stared at him, shook her head and cried even more.

He, too, shook his head and walked over to her garden wall. He took a loose stone from the top of the wall and dropped it into the hole. In that case, he said, why don't you just bury this rock. It's worth just as much as the treasure that you lost and never used.

THE ANT AND THE DOVE

A Dove was standing near a stream when she happened to see an Ant fall into the water. She watched him struggle valiantly but soon saw that the current was much too strong for him to swim to shore and that he would surely soon die. She picked up a nearby piece of straw and flew out over the water, swooped low and close to the Ant, then dropped it within his reach.

Of course he immediately clutched at the straw and held tight until the water carried him to the shore at the next bend in the brook. He did not know how to thank the Dove for her kindness, because Ants do not usually talk to Doves. But he soon found a way.

It happened that a hunter was walking very quietly toward the Dove and her flock where they were feeding peacefully. The Ant watched as the Man prepared to fling a stone at the Dove who had saved his life. Without a thought for his own safety he raced toward the Man, climbed up onto his sandal and bit through the skin of his heel until he felt his pincers touching bone.

The Man yelled and stamped his foot, shaking the dazed Ant into a nearby clump of grass where he lay, unable to move. Maybe he couldn't move, but he could hear and he heard the flock of Doves take to the air and fly to safety. He had returned the favour and saved her life.

BELLING THE CAT

A large family of Mice were gathered in the wall of a house to discuss their life. Many things about life in that house were good. There were always lots of crumbs on the kitchen floor, passages in the walls led from room to room for safe travel and the people in the house never set traps to try to catch them. Life was good except for one thing: the Cat.

Mice are quick and can usually get from room to room or back to their hole in the wall as soon as they see the Cat. But the Cat was also quick, and worse than that, quiet. So it happened that, as good as life was in that house, now and then a Mouse would get caught and eaten by the terrifying big Cat. Sometimes it was a cousin or an old aunt or a silly young Mouse who wouldn't keep a hiding place within reach. There were always lots of Mice and the family was big but they still didn't like it when someone went missing, even if they hardly noticed.

So at this meeting they came to an agreement: the Cat was a Problem. They discussed the Problem over and over to try to understand it and the thing they always came back to was that the Cat was just too quiet. Quick as they were and as good as they were at getting into safe places, they just didn't always know where the Cat was and what she was up to. The Cat was a Problem that needed a Solution.

Suddenly a smart young Mouse, who had only heard about the Cat but had never seen her, came up with a brilliant and simple solution to their problem. "Our biggest problem is that we can't hear the Cat until it's too late," he said. "All we have to do is put a loud bell around the Cat's neck and then we'll hear her even when she's in the next room."

Most of the other Mice patted him on the back thanking him for his fantastic idea. They laughed at themselves for never having thought of it before and at the same time were sad for all the Mice that the Cat had eaten just because they were so stupid.

One old Mouse sat in a corner by herself and watched the others. She had lived in that house all her life and had seen the Cat many times. She only had half a tail (you can guess where the other half went) and was extremely careful whenever she left the hole. "I don't really want to spoil your celebrating," she said, "but which one of you will go out there to put the bell around the Cat's neck?"

TWO TRAVELLERS AND A BEAR

In a far off place and a far off time people did all their travelling on foot. Mostly it was safe to do so because villages were close together and travellers were never alone in the wilderness for very long. But sometimes on longer journeys the spaces between villages were much bigger and so were the chances of meeting dangerous wild animals.

It was on such a journey that two men travelling together met a big black Bear. We hear many different things about what to do if you meet a Bear and one of the men had heard that it's best for two people to stay close together and wave their arms and yell. This might make the Bear think that the two of you are a big, noisy, dangerous creature that he should avoid if possible. So the man started to do this, thinking that his friend would join him and together scare the Bear away.

But his friend had other ideas in his mind. He was so frightened by the Bear walking towards them that he quickly left his friend standing there alone and climbed high into a nearby tree. The Bear, of course, was not afraid of the lone man standing there and kept on walking towards him. The man quickly remembered what else he had heard about Bears and fell to the ground and played dead.

The Bear walked a few wide circles around the "dead" man sniffing at the air and watching carefully to see if he moved. The man lay as still as a tree trunk. The Bear also looked up at the man in the tree whose heart was pounding and whose hands were trembling so badly he could barely hang on.

The Bear began to smell the man all over. He started at his feet. He poked at his legs with his nose, he sniffed up over his hips and onto his back. The man was afraid but he kept himself calm and still. The Bear even rolled him over onto his back, without using his claws, and smelled his belly. The man almost laughed out loud when the Bear poked him in the ribs with his snout. The Bear moved up to the man's head and snuffled in his hair and on his neck. The man didn't once even open his eyes.

From in the tree the other watched, still frozen with his fear. He couldn't believe how long the Bear was staying by his friend's head. It even looked as if the Bear were whispering in his friend's ear. To his surprise, while he was watching, the Bear simply walked away down the path and out of sight. Both men stayed where they were for quite a long time. Finally the man on the ground stood up and the man in the tree climbed down.

"We surely were lucky that the Bear left us alone," said the still trembling man as he reached the ground. "But from where I was watching, it looked as if the Bear whispered something into your ear. Did he?"

"As a matter of fact, he did," replied the man angrily. "He told me I should be more careful about how I choose my friends. He said that a true friend wouldn't have run away from danger and leave me to face it alone."

THE PEACOCK'S TAIL

Long ago, long before this story was ever written down and people only knew of it because they heard it from the mouth of a wandering storyteller, the Peacock had a tail that was as plain and as dull as any other bird's tail. He knew that he wanted something that would make him stand out from the rest of the birds. He wanted something that would make him particularly beautiful. He saw feather crested birds and birds with colours on their wings. He saw birds with frighteningly big claws and birds with beaks that could easily crack the toughest nut. But wherever he looked all he saw were birds with plain tails.

That's it, he thought. If I had the most beautiful tail in the entire bird kingdom, then I would stand out and be noticed by everyone. So he wished and he prayed and he howled and he wailed until somehow his wish came true. He woke up one morning with a tail so long and thick that it flowed to the ground behind him. He lifted his new tail and spread it wide in the sun for all to see. He cried out in his loud, shrill voice to get everyone to look at him. And look they did!

All were amazed at the colours and the patterns and the dazzling beauty of it as he spread it out behind him. But of course they all had to go back about their business and they went on their way. Suddenly he looked up and saw a bird he had never seen before. It was a great eagle who had never before lived in that part of the world.

The peacock watched as the eagle soared high above. He circled slowly, letting the warm winds carry him higher and higher, then he closed his wings and fell like a stone only to open them at the last minute and swoop close to the treetops and climb back high into the sky.

That is the most beautiful thing I have ever seen in my life, the peacock thought. I must do that, too. He spread his wings and ran, flapping as hard as he could. But his tail was far too heavy as it dragged along on the ground behind him. The eagle soared away and was not seen in that land ever again. The peacock tried again but soon realized that his beautiful tail was to forever keep him a prisoner of the ground.

SOUR GRAPES

A Fox on his way from one forest to another crossed through a valley that was rich with people's farms. It was daytime and the fox knew that farmers were always watching much more carefully in the daytime than at night. So he stayed away from the chicken yard which was much too close to the house. He made a wide loop around the duck pond below the garden, even though he knew what duck tasted like. He even snuck carefully past the barnyard and didn't even look at the two day old lamb who bleated frightenedly when his father, the ram, bellowed at the fox disappearing into the cornfield.

There were just too many people around and some of them had guns. The fox soon found that the safest place to cross the valley was through the vineyard. Nobody was working there that day. It was late summer and the vines were heavy with grapes. He ate a few green grapes that were hanging close to the ground. Not bad, he thought as he ate a few more. He ate a few red grapes that he could reach if he stood on his hind legs. Even better, he thought as he ate a few more. He went from red to green and back to red again, enjoying the sweet, juicy grapes that hung warm in the sun.

He soon found himself on a hill at the edge of the vineyard. He saw the other forest he was heading for and was just about to run across the open space and into the safety of the woods when he saw the tallest grape vine he had ever seen. The vines grew up a tall pole and at the top of that pole, shining in the sun, were the biggest, juiciest looking grapes in the whole valley. The fox had liked the green grapes. He had loved the red grapes. These grapes at the top of the pole, were a deep purple that promised a sweetness he had only ever tasted in his dreams.

He licked the drool from his chops and ran greedily to the vine, expecting a very lovely dessert after a very lovely meal. The closer he got, the higher the vine looked. He ate a few deep red grapes from near the bottom. They were excellent. He ate a few light purple grapes from as high as he could reach on his hind feet. They melted in his mouth, the sweet juice gliding down his throat.

He looked at the deep purple grapes hanging high above his head. He was determined to get them. He jumped straight up and didn't even come close. He took a run and jumped hard and landed with a few leaves in his mouth. He tried to clamber up the vine but only fell back into the dirt. Again and again he ran and jumped and ran and jumped until he was too tired to jump again.

Bah! he said, as he turned his back on the grapes. I'm sure they are sour anyway. Who needs needs them, he thought bitterly as he walked into the forest without looking back.

SOUR GRAPES

The Fox, that wily beast!
Saw some grapes. What a feast! he thought,
And walked to where they hung on the vine.
The grapes that grew below,
He soon swallowed, don't you know about
The ones the farmer wanted for wine?

They're pretty good, he thought.
I could surely eat the lot of them,
Especially those that hang up so high.
They're big, they're round, they're sweet.
They will be my special treat and I
Can surely jump that high up if I try.

He looked, he aimed, he sprang.
He fell short and shouted DANG! but then
He jumped again as hard as he could.
Eleven times he tried.
On the twelfth he turned aside and said:
They're sour anyway, and no good.

THE LION AND THE MOUSE

A Lion lay asleep in the forest,
He knew naught of fear or of dread.
A daydreaming Mouse out a-roaming,
Accident-al-ly stepped on his head.

The Lion with a paw quick as lightning,
Pinned the terrified Mouse to the ground.
"Let me go, Sire, I'll surely repay you,
When some day, deep in trouble you're found."

The roar of the Lion shook the forest,
As he laughed at the Mouse 'neath his paw.
"You're a fool little Mouse, but I like you.
Tell your friends of my teeth that you saw!"

Much later the Lion was hunting,
But was caught in a human-made snare.
The roar of his anger was fearsome.
Yet his struggles? They got him nowhere.

The Mouse hurried off to the roaring,
Where the Lion in bondage now lay.
And he chewed and he gnawed through the bindings,
And with freedom a kindness repaid.

BELLING THE CAT

The Mice once called a meeting
To decide upon a plan.
The Cat, their lifelong enemy,
From whom they always ran,
Was terrorizing all Mousekind,
All day and all night through.
When finally one smart, young Mouse
Squeaked "I know what to do!"

The plan was simple, oh so sweet,
Around her neck they'd hang,
A bell so bold and brassy it
Would warn them with its clang.
"How dense we've been to wait so long.
Before we *thought* of that!"
But one old wise and wary Mouse
Asked: "Who will bell the Cat?"

THE BUNDLE OF STICKS

A farmer had three daughters,
With whom he shared his land.
They worked the fields together
With head and heart and hand.

But they began to quarrel,
Each thought that she was right.
They argued how to farm the land.
Instead of work, they'd fight.

The father watched his daughters,
Their actions brought him harm.
He feared their constant bickering
Would make them lose the farm.

One day the old man noticed
His time of Death was near.
He called the three together,
His wisdom for to hear.

Three sticks were tied together,
A bundle tight and strong.
He asked each one to break it,
And each tried hard and long.

But none could break the bundle,
No matter how she tried.
The father then removed the strings,
The sticks lay spread, untied.

To each he gave a single branch,
And said: make short its length.
As each stick snapped, they understood,
In unity is strength.

TWO TRAVELLERS AND A BEAR

Two men were walking in the woods,
One bright and sunny day.
When suddenly a big brown bear
Surprised them on their way.

Perhaps together they could scare
The bear away with yelling.
But one man quickly climbed a tree,
With fear his heart was swelling.

The second man fell to the ground
And lay as still as stone.
For he had heard a bear will leave
A dead man quite alone.

The bear approached and sniffed the man,
Yes, touched him with his nose.
He smelled his hands, he smelled his back,
He even smelled his toes.

He snuffled on the "dead" man's neck,
And lingered by his ear.
From in the tree the other watched,
Still frozen with his fear.

The bear, not hungry, went away.
The man called from the tree.
It seemed the bear was whispering.
What did he say to thee?

He said I must be wary,
Of one who calls me friend,
But runs away at danger,
And no helping hand will lend.

THE MISER

A miserly old woman
Had a secret bag of gold,
Hidden buried in her garden near a tree.

It was her precious treasure
Which she loved to touch and hold,
And each day she'd dig it up and dance with glee.

A thief so cold and cunning,
From behind the garden wall,
Was observing what the stingy miser did.

He waited there with patience
Till he saw the darkness fall,
Then he dug it, stole it, ran away and hid.

Her screams of pain and horror
Could be heard in all the town,
As she found her treasure missing from its place.

A neighbour asked her kindly,
What had been inside the ground?
And she told him all, with sadness on her face.

But money is for spending
On the things we need each day,
Said the neighbour when he heard what she had told.

Then he tossed a rock into the hole
And went upon his way,
Saying: Bury that, it's just as good as gold.

THE PEACOCK

In the days of old, when the Peacock bold,
Was not a splendid bird.
He begged, he wailed for a pretty tail,
And soon his prayers were heard.

With feathers of light, that shone so bright,
He strutted tall and proud.
Not even the pheasant, looked so pleasant!
He stood out in a crowd.

Till one day he, looked up to see,
An eagle soaring high.
He got in his mind, to be of that kind,
And he flapped his wings to fly.

But that grand tail, like a great ship's sail,
Did keep him on the ground.
And until this day, it has stayed that way.
In his beauty he's Earthbound.

THE ANT AND THE DOVE

A Dove saw an Ant falling into a brook,
And she watched as he struggled to swim.
She dropped him a straw which he managed to hook.
And he floated to shore with a grin.

The Ant saw a hunter take aim with a stone,
That was meant for his saviour, the Dove.
So he bit the man's foot, driving clear to the bone,
And repaid her first kindness with love.

And finally a collection of stories triggered by many different impulses and inspirations.

WRITING STORIES

Our memories are our source material for fictional stories. Every story, from the shortest vignette to the longest multi-volume epic, has its roots in the author's mind and memory. Of course each story gets transformed every time it is told, whether orally or on paper. This transformation is the key to artistic freedom: I don't need to retell events in their exact sequence; I can add or delete characters, streets or settings at will; I can use a memory of five seconds to become the basis of a tale told over ten years.

The following is a personal illustration of how a memory became the springboard into a story about children who have only lived in the minds of the author and his readers.

THE MEMORY

It was an unusually hot day in May in the mountains. My brother Mike and I and a couple of friends, both of whom happened to be named Ken, headed up into the hills looking for adventure and respite from the heat. We found both in full measure.

We knew of many old tunnels in the surrounding mountains so we armed ourselves with candles and flashlights and set out. We went to a mine named "Snowball." We had been in there before but never farther than the daylight penetrated.

We formed a single file and went in. The air was cool and stale and smelled of old, damp rock. After rounding two corners, perhaps a hundred yards in, we had forgotten how hot it was outside and were even wishing we had brought jackets. The tunnel was high enough that we could walk standing straight but I noticed that we all tended to hunch as we walked, not wanting to bang our heads on the jagged, granite ceiling.

Around the next corner we heard a chorus of plinking water drops, dripping like a hundred leaky faucets. We trained our lights forward and saw a forest of two foot ice trees sprouting from the tunnel floor. Directly above them was a mirror image of icicles hanging from the arched surface of the stone ceiling. From each stalactite fell a slow steady drip landing in the hollowed, water-filled tip of its stalagmite partner. It was a magical sight. Spring was late in coming to this underground wonderland. A half a mile of bedrock insulation would protect the the ice forest till well into the summer.

We carefully made our way through and continued down the again dry tunnel. Ken V. suggested we shut off the lights and try to go in the dark. The intensity of the darkness startled us at first and we all stood there silently, probably with our mouths open. Try as we might, we saw nothing. There was no light.

We spent a few hours in that mine, refusing the temptation of old, rotting catwalks that spanned gaping, black pits, tossing rocks down seemingly bottomless vertical shafts and merely sitting around a candle eating oranges, awed by where we were. On our way out we went down a side tunnel just to see where it led. Around the first corner we saw something that shocked us: light.

It was an air vent leading to the surface at about a sixty degree angle. It looked to be about forty or fifty feet to the top. Ken A. and Mike didn't want to try it. Ken V. and I did. We agreed to meet at the main entrance.

It was narrow and steep but the rough-hewn rock provided good grips. We both made it.

THE STORY

THE FORGOTTEN MINE

"Gee, I wish the swimming pool was open," said Teddy to his friends, Bill and Andy. It was an unusually hot Saturday in May as the boys sat under a flowering apple tree in Andy's back yard.

"Let's go for a hike," suggested Bill who was tired of sitting and tired of hearing about the heat.

"Great idea, Bill," declared Andy. "We could go exploring the old mine roads above the town."

"My Uncle Phil said they used to go way back into the mines with flashlights and stuff when he was a kid," said Teddy.

"Yeah, but they're all sealed up now," added Andy. "Too many tunnels were starting to cave in."

"Who knows?" asked Bill, itching for action. "Maybe they forgot some."

"I'll go get a canteen of water," said Andy as he made for the back door. "I'll meet you guys out front."

Andy filled his scout canteen and stuffed it into his day pack along with three oranges. Maybe Bill was right, he thought. Who knows? He opened a cupboard and took out three candles and a box of matches and added them to the pack.

The unseasonal heat sent the three seventh graders up to where the fir and spruce forest offered unlimited shade and secret places to discover. The remnants of a long abandoned mining road lured them deep into the forest, growing fainter the further they went. The track ended suddenly and they found themselves standing before the open mouth of a tunnel.

"Hey, Bill, you were right. They did forget to close up this one," said Andy as he and Bill pressed forward, eager to go into the mine.

"Wait a minute, you guys," warned Teddy. "My uncle said these old mines are pretty dangerous."

"What's the matter? Are you chicken?" scoffed Bill

"No, just careful," retorted Teddy.

"Hey look, you two," exclaimed Andy soothingly. "If we take it easy and watch what we're doing, then there's nothing to worry about."

"Wow, it's cooler already," said Teddy, only a few yards in.

"Yeah, and what a weird smell," added Bill. "The air is so stale."

A couple of dozen paces brought the boys to the end of the wedge of daylight that impotently challenged the darkness. "There's not much light back here," remarked Andy, looking back at the bright archway of the opening.

Bill rounded the first corner, feeling the rusty, narrow gauge railroad track with his feet. "Man, it's dark," he said. "We should have brought a flashlight."

"Maybe this will help," said Andy as he struck a match and held it against a candle wick.

The boys continued, ducking instinctively even though the ceiling was a foot above their heads. They inspected the rotting timbers that had been placed more than half a century earlier to brace the walls and ceiling. They ventured briefly into side tunnels, not wanting to leave the security of the iron rails that connected them with the outside.

They had been walking for close to five minutes and were becoming nervously aware of the distance between them and daylight. Suddenly they heard a low, muffled drumming like distant thunder coming from the tunnel far behind them. A rush of wind met them as they turned to look.

"What was that?" gasped Bill.

They all knew, but nobody wanted to say it.

"I think we should get out of here," said Teddy.

They soon came to a cloud of choking dust as thick as the darkness. They pushed forward holding the candle close to the floor. Bill, in the lead, stumbled and fell painfully over a jumble of loose rock. The candle went out.

"Nnngg, owww," moaned Bill in the dark, clutching his bruised knee.

"Light another candle, Andy" said Teddy.

Andy and Teddy helped Bill to his feet and inspected the rubble with the light of two candles. The pile reached the ceiling.

"We're trapped," shouted Bill, scrabbling furiously with his hands, trying to burrow his way out.

"Cut it out, Bill!" ordered Andy. "You'll only make it worse."

"I can't breathe," coughed Bill, his fear turning to panic.

A deep groan from the walls sounded around them making them feel the mountain was angry with these trespassers. A second, louder rumble thundered through the mountain shaking dust and stones down upon the three boys. "We have to go back," said Andy. He grabbed Bill by the arm and pulled hard, forcing him deeper into the tunnel. They ran crouched with arms stretched forward, straining in the dim light to see ahead.

"Down this way," called Andy, ducking into a side tunnel.

"Hey, you guys, do you smell that?" asked Teddy.

"What?" panted Bill.

"Fresh air. I smell fresh air!"

They hurried forward, cheered by the chance of escape. What met them around the next corner took them all by surprise that quickly turned to glee. "Light, light!" shouted Andy, pointing ahead.

A broad beam of daylight fell to the floor. The three boys peered into the hole at the top of the tunnel wall and saw a circle of blue sky at the end of the air vent that angled up through the rock to freedom.

A STORY OF "ONE"

"What is the biggest number, Dad?" The little girl was busy counting and saw that the numbers just kept getting bigger and bigger.

"Oh, a thousand," said her father who was reading the newspaper and didn't really hear the question anyway or see how important it was to his daughter.

"No, a thousand isn't the biggest! I know that a million is the biggest and that Tony said a billion is even bigger than that. What's bigger than a billion?"

"A trillion," he said absently.

She was amazed to think that anything could be bigger than a billion. Billion was a word she had heard from older children and they had told her that she could never count to a billion. Now her father had told her that there was a number called a trillion that was even bigger than a billion.

Surely a trillion is the biggest number, she thought. She had a bag of marbles she was counting out. She counted and counted and counted until they ran out and it was around eighty somewhere. But if I were to just keep on counting I could count all the rest of my toys and my bears and my clothes and my dresser and my bed and all the forks and knives in the kitchen. Surely if I counted all the things in our house I would reach the biggest number.

Something in her wouldn't let her quit thinking about it. She thought about the world around her with all the things in it. Houses, cars, people, mountains, lakes. *(An excellent chance to let the children contribute to the story)*

I could never count everything. Nobody could. EVERYTHING is too much to count. It has too many parts in it. More parts than that big puzzle that Mama made.

Like a flash she saw a picture of EVERYTHING, of ALL THAT IS and that all the things of the world and beyond were parts of it. EVERYTHING is everything, she thought. There is only one EVERYTHING. She was very excited. It seemed even more exciting than discovering a cave. EVERYTHING is one and it has millions and billions and trillions of parts. EVERYTHING is ONE. One is everything.

EVERYTHING must be the biggest number because if you count everything and really don't leave anything out, then you can't count any higher. If everything is ONE and EVERYTHING is everything and the biggest number, then the biggest number must be **ONE!**

HO TIN, RICE PLANTER

The sun was not yet up, the day was not yet bright, but still Ho Tin was wakened by her mother and asked to get ready for another day in the rice paddies. The paddies were in the great tracts of flat land below the village along the Mekong River. The wet, hot season was here and the young, tender shoots of rice had to be planted into the mud of the paddies before the true heat of summer came.

Ho Tin was the youngest daughter of the Ho family in the village of Thum on the banks of the river called Mekong (called simply the River by all who lived near it) in the country called Cambodia. As in many lands in that part of the world called Southeast Asia, Ho Tin and her family and all the villagers ate mainly rice and their work was mainly with the rice. Ho Tin was seven years old and this was her third season working in the rice paddies.

The priests of the village had brought the tiny seedling plants of rice that were to be carefully, one by one, placed in the mud. She had seen the priests in their ceremonial white robes bringing the hand-high shoots to the women waiting at the edge of the paddy. The priests had sown the best seeds of last year's harvest in special beds of earth. Their chants and prayers had gone out to the creator as thanks for the harvest and as an asking for another good season of growth. Now the sprouts were delicate little plants ready for the flooded fields.

Ho Tin's mother and sisters, as well as many other women and girls of the village now worked with backs bent, carefully pressing the roots into the soft mud. The water lapped gently around their ankles. They walked backwards slowly as their hands worked quickly with the shoots.

The men of the village, those who were not fishing, scooped out the mud that had settled in the canals to keep the waterways free. The mud was poured into large wooden tubs which stood nearby. Other men and boys carried manure from the village to stir into the tubs. There were very few animals in the village but the solid waste of the people's toilet buckets was carefully mixed with whatever animal manure could be gathered. When the smelly mixture was thin enough to scoop with a ladle, Ho Tin filled a bucket and carefully gave each plant its share of the brown liquid that would give life to the plant and because of that, to the village. The manure settled into the mud around each tiny plant.

The water from the river was controlled with canals. Too much water would drown the plants. Too little water would cause the plants to dry out and die. The villagers knew their work well; they had learned it from their elders who also had learned from theirs. The knowledge was part of the life of the village and had been for many, many generations. They knew not only exactly how much water needed to be let into the paddies from the river, but also how fast the water could flow through the canals and around the plants, for it was in this slowly moving water that the rice grew best.

Day after day the rice grew. The plants were cared for, fed, replaced when necessary. They grew tall and strong and when the flowering was finished the dams on the lower end of the field were opened and the water was allowed to flow out of the paddies and back into the river.

The grains grew fat and the heat of the tropical sun ripened them. Just as the priests had played an important part in the sowing of the rice, so too did ancient traditions guide the people through the harvest. The harvest was a time of silence. As long as the rice was being cut there was no laughing or talking. When the harvest was finished, the villagers celebrated the food and seed they had for another year.

Rice was Ho Tin's work, her food, her world and her life.

HOUSE OF MIRRORS

I was just ready to leave the amusement park when I saw the sign HOUSE OF MIRRORS on a trailer between the monkeys and the woman with a hundred tattoos. I paid my quarter and stepped inside. In the first room was a green door and a single, full length mirror, like in clothing store try-on rooms. There must be more, I thought, and went through the door. In the next room was a yellow door and two large mirrors. I stood in front of one and laughed out loud at what looked back. I saw a dwarf, perhaps one metre tall and just as wide. He laughed back at me and his broad, flat face grew even wider as I leaned towards him. Curious, I turned around and saw a creature as thin as a pencil who looked just like me. As I moved towards him his body bent and spread, his head grew large, then flat, then stretched diagonally from temple to jaw. I played a while longer with these caricatures of me then walked to the yellow door. The next room was full of people, all of them me. I saw me from behind, I saw me beside myself, I saw endless columns of me stretching off into infinity. They looked in every direction. Some looked at me. I took a step. They all moved. Some disappeared, others took their place. New ones looked at me, watching and waiting curiously for my next move. I put my hand on my face. A hundred, a thousand hands came up to mimic me. I opened my mouth and saw a thousand tongues framed by twenty-thousand teeth. I closed one eye. A thousand cyclopses stared at a thousand things. I closed my other eye and was alone.

MOUNTAIN SUMMER

I plodded slowly up the steep, narrow road, head down, watching the dust as it exploded from beneath my feet to settle in layers on my once clean boots. Sweat ran in trickles from my forehead, tracing cooling lines down cheek and nose, then dropped soundlessly into the inch deep dust. The searing August sun baked the south facing mountain slope where the abandoned mining road climbed snakelike to the sealed entrance of the long closed goldmine.

The road levelled suddenly under my lowered head. I looked up to face the heavy steel door welded tight on top and sides. The dull, black, rust-inhibiting paint was chipped and marred in a hundred places by the thrown stones of decades of frustrated young explorers. The narrow gauge railroad tracks jutted two feet from beneath the door like the broken tusks of some great defeated beast lying facedown in the dust. The rails shed flakes of rust that melted into the surrounding earth with a reddish hue that reminded me of pulverized bricks.

I had known of it and other tunnels for many years. I had been told of the dangers that existed before the county sealed the mines thirty years ago. Stories of lost children, trapped miners and crazy recluses added to the fascination and lure that called from behind that impenetrable barrier. Hands and knees in the dust, I peered under the door seeing only the rapidly diminishing wedge of light that impotently challenged the darkness.

I thrust a hand gropingly under the door, felt the cool, still air that hung only a forearm's length away. The cool air and cooler stones of the tunnel floor increased my longing for respite from the dusty heat in which I sat. The black iron door radiated heat, forcing me back.

A slow, uncooling draught fell from the mountainside, heavy with the scent of dry pine needles and parched ferns, the smells of a hot mountain summer. The rattle of the remaining few drops in my water bottle told me I must leave soon, but I lingered, not yet ready to admit defeat.

Again I went to the door, bowing obediently to squint into the blackness that filled the tunnel. I listened, smelled, for some clue of what lay beyond. A very distant tick-tick-tick of dripping water, like the slow, regular heartbeat of a sleeping giant, made me lick my drying lips as I imagined a black, bottomless pool at the core of the mountain. Subtle scents rose gently in my nose as I closed my eyes and pulled slowly at the dark mysterious air. Mingling with the hot dryness of the outside earth came odours like those of old, decaying mushrooms, damp, slime-covered stone and some faint essence that spoke of animal musk. Bats and rats, I thought, as I opened my eyes.

The sun scorching my back, the iron door fever hot against my face, I rose slowly and shook my head to clear it of visions of that hidden, secret place. I moved backwards, dragging my feet a dozen paces through the dust, still gripped by the desire to see beyond that door. I picked up a stone the size of my fist and flung it at the centre of the door. A shiny new fleck appeared among the hundred other weathered scars and the door sounded its taunting, metallic laugh as I turned and walked away.

A BITE OF PIZZA

I'm going to take you on a journey, like none you've ever been on before. You've all been on a journey before, like to Chattanooga or Spokane or maybe even to Budapest or Toronto or Australia or Africa. But this is a journey we will take without even leaving the classroom. Some of you might think that the places on this journey are a little yucky because this journey starts in your mouth, goes through lots of other damp, dark places and ends up . . . oh we'll get to that.

Yes, this journey is going to be about a piece of food making its way through your body. Let's make it something nobody likes to eat, just for fun. Something like pizza. We could go on and on about making or buying the pizza but let's just start with a nice juicy first bite. We people (and many animals, too) are very complicated and most of what happens inside of us happens without us even knowing it, or at least without us really controlling it. Those things that happen on their own are called involuntary reactions. The actual biting down on the pizza is a voluntary action; we do that consciously. But everything that happens after that just happens.

Okay, let's take that bite! Ooompfff!!!!! We immediately start chewing and that is a real mix of voluntary and involuntary action. We can control it if we want to but it can also just keep on happening without us thinking about it much. But what we can't really control, and what begins happening right away is the production of saliva. Yes, your saliva glands start spewing out spit like fountains. Your teeth, mostly the big grinding molars in the back, crush the bite of pizza and mix it with the saliva.

That saliva, or spit, is actually pretty complicated stuff. It has several jobs to do before you swallow the bite of pizza. The first is just to get it wet. Try to imagine swallowing a piece of dry bread. Of course you can't. The saliva gets it wet so it can slide around better in your mouth. Spit also helps you to taste your food. But probably the most important job spit does is chemical. Saliva is not just water. It is made of stuff that helps your body digest the food it mixes with. Think of that piece of pizza. Most of it is crust, which you probably know is called starch or carbohydrates. Well saliva starts right away to break starch down. It turns it into sugar!

So now that first bite of pizza is all mixed up with saliva and is a wet ball of mush. The tongue then pushes it to the back of your mouth, a trap door opens, the stuff slides through and down it goes. Swallowing is another one of those involuntary actions. Once that trap door closes your body just takes over. The tube that goes down into your stomach is called the esophagus and it is lined with muscles all the way down. These muscles squeeze the chewed up pizza kind of like squeezing a tube of toothpaste until the stuff reaches the bottom. At the bottom there's a valve that is forced open by the food coming down. The chewed up, slimy lump of stuff that used to be a piece of pizza squeezes through the valve and drops into your stomach.

Now try to imagine being that bite of pizza down there in your stomach. You would not like where you are! You're in a big pink muscular bag being sloshed around in a sea of mush. Acid is raining down on you. It's a very powerful acid. The only reason the bag doesn't get totally destroyed by the acid is because the walls of your stomach are coated with a thick, sticky mucus that protects them from the acid. But the bite of pizza does get all mixed up with the acid and breaks down into finer and finer pieces.

Remember I told you that the stomach was a muscular bag? Well those muscles are really working. They are turning and churning the pizza, folding it over, squeezing it, massaging it not very gently at all. It's almost like a washing machine in there and the stuff that used to be pizza is getting broken down into a fine creamy mush that has had a lot of liquid added to it and is now thin and watery.

Your pizza is about to move into a new part of your body but let's have a quick look at the time it has taken since you first bit into it until now. The bite itself probably took about two seconds. Fast chewers swallow as soon as five seconds later but then the food isn't properly mixed with the juices from the mouth, and that makes the stomach work harder later. Good chewing should take twenty to thirty seconds. The swallow itself is really interesting because it starts with a very powerful muscle movement that forces the food through the pharynx at the amazing speed of twenty-five feet per second. The rest of the squeeze down through the esophagus takes about ten seconds. So from the time you took that bite until the food is actually in your stomach about a half a minute has passed.

Then things really slow down. So if you are the kind of person who likes to get the trip over with, this is not the journey for you. It takes three to four hours for the stomach to finish its churning and squashing and sloshing and liquefying and that's where we are now in our journey.

By this time the food doesn't look at all like it did a few hours ago. It is a thin, watery substance called chyme, which gets squeezed through another valve, kind of like a round doorway, into the small intestine. Now there is a strange place! It's a tight, watery tunnel or tube that goes back and forth and back and forth all squished up against large intestines below and the stomach above and the other organs all around. Some of those organs, like the kidneys and pancreas, get into the act at this point and send liquids and chemicals into the chyme that mix in and help us use the food.

But this tube isn't hollow like a garden hose with water flowing through it. Inside the small intestine are thousands and thousands of tiny fingers that stick from the walls of the intestine into the chyme that is passing through. These fingers are called villi and look like tiny cactuses but they are really like tiny sponges reaching into the chyme to pull all the good things out of the food so our bodies can use it as energy.

This is where the food we eat becomes the fuel to run the wonderful thing that is our body so we can do things like run and talk and think and laugh and lift and throw and eat again so we can start all over.

Those little spongy fingers soak all the energy, what we call nutrients, out of the food and bring it to our blood, which then carries it to every part of the body. The story of how the blood circulates throughout our whole body is really interesting, but that story is for another day.

This is another part of the journey that is rather slow. It takes about three hours for our liquefied pizza to travel through the small intestine and all the time it is sending its energy out through the villi to run our bodies. By the time the goop reaches the end of the small intestine all the good stuff has been taken out of it and it is time for the body to keep it moving and get rid of it.

You thought parts of the journey were slow up until now! The next stage of the trip can take anywhere from half a day to two days. The chyme gets forced out of the small intestine into the large intestine. The job of the large intestine is basically to dry out the chyme. The body has used up all the goodies and now it's time to recycle the water. The water gets soaked out through the walls of the large intestine, also called the colon, and used up by the body before it gets peed out. The further the stuff travels through the large intestine the drier it gets. What's left is garbage and it's only about one third the size of the original food it started as.

There's one more place for the stuff to go. It's called the rectum. Once the pizza reaches the rectum it is no longer recognizable as pizza. It is a solid mass in various handsome shades of brown. The rectum sends signals to the brain, which is another story of its own, and we get the message loud and clear which sounds something like: "I really have to take a poo."

The last part of the journey is very close now. The brown mass, which we call feces and which has lots of other names as well, is squeezed out through another of those many doorways it has gone through. This one is called the anus and where the stuff goes from there is another story.

So there you have it. It was a journey that took from one to two days and in a grown up the distance travelled was only about twenty-five feet, or about seven or eight metres. If you live to be an old man or woman, by the time you are that age you will have sent about fifty tons of food on that journey.

OTHERS WALKED

He dreamed that he was reading. It was a disjointed sort of dream, the kind that fascinate and confuse. He was reading of a journey or a wandering. The destination was unclear or unknown. He saw the sentence and read on until it pulled it him back. It was a short sentence. *Others walked.* Two words. He looked again at it and felt something: a touch, excitement?

It was a simple sentence. *Others walked.* He searched for the source of his fascination. It lay there before him but was somehow covered, nebulous. He looked harder, concentrating on the words that gripped his mind and caused gentle currents in his spine. He knew the words, understood their meaning, this context. Yet still he looked at that short, simple sentence. The writer's device to catch the eye. make a point, a statement?

The reading metamorphosed into his normal dreaming of pictures, of people doing what they do, of living. There were a great many people, all moving in more or less the same direction. Some were in automobiles, some were on wagons drawn by horses or oxen. Some moved very quickly—he could not tell how. *Others walked.* Why were these others walking? And to where? They were fewer than those around them. And much slower. Who were they? Why the word *others*? It implied a difference, even an anomaly. Even dreaming, he wondered at his own fascination. He was not a walker; a mile or two if necessary.

He woke. The haunting power of the dream stayed with him, hindering his return to sleep. He recalled the dream and the hold it had on his dream self. He quickly, quietly, pulled on his clothes, his shoes. He walked till dawn. He reached the edge of the city: at least three hours and probably ten miles. He knew what he was doing but not why. He turned and walked back, puzzled at his actions, aware of fatigue in his legs.

He reached his room and lay thankfully on his bed. The dream returned, the same page, the same words. *Others walked.*

He woke again, tried to get up and was quickly reminded of his early morning walk. It was evening now and he was late for work. There was something pleasant about the pain and stiffness in his legs. I walked twenty miles this morning, he thought. He laughed. He ate and prepared to go to his evening job. He stood at the corner, the bus came and he watched it leave again. I'm late already, he thought, and he walked.

I know I'm late, he said calmly. No, it won't happen again. After midnight the walk home from work relaxed him. Sleep came quickly. And morning.

He thought of the days spent at home, waiting for the time to go to his job, of reading, wasting time, drinking and smoking a bit, of convincing himself he was enjoying the music, visiting friends, exchanging banalities, of deeper friendships and relationships never lasting. He recalled his pleasure at avoiding the fast pace of the day. He remembered the countless bus rides through the dying streets of the city after rush hour. It felt different today. Coffee and cigarette left him unsatisfied. Strange, he thought. Restless he could not sit in front of the television.

The morning light was hard on his unaccustomed eyes. Where to?, he thought as he walked down the sidewalk away from the city's heart. He took the same route as yesterday's dawn, clinging to the familiar. The day brightened and it was good. He saw children playing in the street, flower gardens and dark green lawns, gravel in the concrete. Amazed at how the city stopped, country began, he continued down an unpaved road.

Something was pulling him—back. I'm hungry, thought. And tired. He had forgotten his cigarettes. He stopped and looked up the road ahead, turned around and faced the city and walked home. He wondered at his actions. He felt better after a shower, a meal, a cigarette. Almost time to catch the bus, he thought.

The faces on the bus were indifferent, uncaring. Where are they going, he thought. His stop came quickly. He was acutely aware of the sameness of his work. This could be last week, he thought. Or last year. Midnight came slowly. He watched the bus pass him and again walked home.

He tried but could not sleep. There was something nagging him, not showing itself but very real. His thoughts turned and spun and slid past his introspective eye not allowing him to fix on them, leaving him no peace. He lay awake all night and got up angry and depressed. Breakfast didn't help: the fried eggs were a heaviness the coffee wouldn't wash away. He stared at the wall, wondering what to do. He walked the few blocks to his neighbourhood tavern, to the back wall and sat facing the door. Shots and chaser relaxed his body, stirred his anger. His reason told him to leave. He listened.

His friend was home, others there, too. Good, he thought. He needed to talk. They agreed with him completely, this city did suck. Yes, their jobs smelled the same as his. Here, have another beer. No? Their laughter sounded ugly.

He walked downtown, peering into windows and faces. The tower sounded noon as he flowed with the crowd across the street. The bookstore had no answers. He could feel his fatigue, his legs, the liquor. He caught a bus to his neighbourhood and sprawled on his bed.

Waking, he refused to hurry to work. And was on time. He noticed small things, things he taken for granted. His co-workers' faces and voices became clear, individual. He went about his routine carefully, making certain all was right. At midnight he told his boss he would not be back.

Sand, fine dust and mud, grass and knee-deep crackling leaves. Coarse rock, freeways, snow and ice, moss, boardwalks and countless forgotten main streets. Shore and steppe, talus and trail, stubble fields and furrows; parched earth, clover, slick pine needles, clay, gravel. Weeks, months, miles, became spans of time and distance without meaning. He crossed deserts and mountain ranges, fought bog and brush till it was no longer a fight. He experienced exhaustion, joy, mindlessness; learned acceptance, strength.

His legs no longer complained of the demands he made. They craved the movement. They were inured to long days, even nights with little rest. They became *they*. He thought of them as entities apart from himself. His mind, his hands, were his conscious self. His legs were his partners—acting on his instructions, yet independent, with a voice in the decisions of the day. He listened carefully to their needs, knowing they were his survival.

On occasion he recalled the dream. Memory of it was vague but he knew it was from a time before. His life's course had been in waves. He had been propelled from a trough by his decision to leave the city. He viewed the undulations of his past as if from a plateau and he saw his future sloping gradually to an obscured, distant height. At times his mind told him that he was chasing a dream, alluring but unobtainable. His legs retorted that it was far better than chasing a bus and the argument ended. Walking had become more than an activity or an enthusiasm. It was a need, a profound physical addiction that he chose to satisfy, knowing it was becoming more deeply rooted.

The trees came slowly to meet him as he walked on the dry, springy duff of the forest floor. He greeted each tree silently as it swept by. Sticks avoided his feet, stones placed themselves comfortably, securely under his soles. Logs fell away and passed beneath him. He was attentive to the silent, still celebration around him. His eyes knew the shapes, the shadows, the light. His ears heard the silence. His legs and feet fondly felt the texture and impact of each step as the ground rose to caress him.

NOTHING'S IMPOSSIBLE

As the pick-up stopped in front of the large, simple ranch house, Heddi Brown and her son Jim stepped from the house to meet their awaited guests.

"Welcome, boys," said Aunt Heddi warmly. "It's good to have you here. We're very glad you could come and stay with us."

"Well, when Uncle Bob wrote and told us he'd need a couple of extra hands this summer, we could hardly wait for school to end," said Tony, speaking for himself and his twin brother Art.

Art turned to his uncle as he heard the driver's door close. "Thanks again for picking us up at the station, Uncle Bob."

"Think nothing of it," replied Bob.

They greeted their cousin Jim who led them hauling their bags to the room the twins would share for the next few months.

"You'll be working with me and Alex," explained Jim as the boys unpacked their suitcases on the twin beds. "Alex is a rider Dad hired for the summer. You'll have to get used to him."

"What do you mean? asked Art.

"Oh, don't get me wrong," said Jim. "I like Alex fine. He just takes a little getting used to."

"What do you mean?" repeated Tony.

"He's as good a cowboy as you'll find anywhere. But he's so darn quiet that he takes some getting used to. He's never unfriendly or anything," continued Jim, "but he never talks about himself. He's hard to get to know." Jim glanced at the twins, then at the door, and whispered conspiratorially behind his hand, "In fact, I call him the *Stranger.*"

Art and Tony had ridden before but they had a lot to learn. They had two good teachers in their cousin Jim and Alex, the *Stranger.* Jim was only two years their senior but had grown up in the saddle and, at eighteen, could handle almost any riding situation. They didn't know where Alex was from but his skill with the reins and the cattle proved him to be a master at all aspects of ranch work. Art and Tony took to the work naturally, watching, doing, learning. The days were long and tiring and the nights of relaxing at the farmhouse were always welcome.

"Well boys," said Uncle Bob one Friday evening after the usual good, hearty meal. "You've been here a month now. How would you like to go into town and spend some of that hard-earned money?"

"There's a travelling carnival in Fontain for the weekend," added Aunt Heddi. "Rides, games, shows, the works. You interested?"

"You bet!" said Tony and Art together, already half out of their chairs.

"Whoa now," laughed their uncle. "I meant tomorrow morning."

Alex elected to stay at the ranch. "Got some riding to do," he had said.

After breakfast the whole family piled into the pick-up and drove the fifteen miles to Fontain. The amusement park was set up in a large field next to the town's grain elevator. Art studied the tall wooden structure as the truck came to a halt. He had always been fascinated by these elevators that were often the most important and almost always the highest building in small prairie towns like Fontain. He hoped for the chance to see the inside of the elevator, too.

"Let's go," said Tony. "That carnival isn't going to wait for us."

Art returned from his reverie and climbed from the truck to join his brother and his cousin as they headed for the entrance to the amusement park. The boys spent the morning watching animal shows, thrilling to the numerous rides and testing their skill at the games they were sure were rigged.

Over lunch the family discussed plans for the afternoon. "Jim and I have to go back to the ranch to do the chores," said Bob. "I'll come back and pick you up around five."

"Why don't the rest of us take in the movie matinee that's playing in town," suggested Aunt Heddi.

"Good idea," said Tony." Besides, it looks as if we're in for one of those summer storms." He pointed to a bank of imposing, dark clouds ascending from the western horizon.

"You two go ahead," said Art. "I'm too restless to sit." He saw his chance to explore the grain elevator he had seen coming into town. "I'd rather just wander around a bit. If that storm hits I'll take cover somewhere."

Art did wander around and the storm did hit. It approached with such speed and struck with such fury that Art was forced to find shelter in the nearest available place. The elevator seemed deserted as Art entered the tiny, windowless room that served as an office. Then he heard the doors closing in the back on the track side of the building: the elevator operator had slammed home the bar to lock the big double doors of the loading bay. Art walked to the back to announce his presence only to find that the doors had been locked from the outside. By the time Art returned to the front the unseen operator, running to avoid a total soaking, had padlocked the entrance and made for his truck, unaware that anyone was inside the building.

Art explored the large, dark building, looking for another way out. Climbing a long spiral staircase he discovered a big, square door that was locked from the inside with a hook. The door was there to accommodate the loading of trains that used the tracks beside the elevator. He had found a way out, but it had one drawback: there were no stairs to the ground three storeys down.

The rain pounded the roof with the staccato of a hundred snare drums. Lightning flashed and the thunderclaps seemed alarmingly close. Art returned to the ground floor and hoped that the lightning came no closer. He had seen the lightning rod atop the elevator and trusted its protection, even in a storm of this intensity.

Then the impossible happened. Two lightning bolts struck the building simultaneously. One hit the lightning rod, its fearsome power conducted harmlessly into the ground. The second smashed into the roof where ridge met rafter, sending splinters and sparks into the dry interior.

The fire spread slowly, hampered by the heavy rain. Smoke billowed from the roof and the wet wood hissed. Art searched the building for another exit or a means to lower himself from the third storey door. Finding neither he returned to that door that opened into space. The distance seemed greater as he contemplated the drop to the gravel below.

Art watched anxiously as the fire spread to an adjoining wall. Precious minutes passed and his fear changed to near panic. He called out, hoping to attract somebody from the town, but the streets were empty and all windows were tight against the wind and rain. Soon he would have to face the flames or jump to the ground.

Suddenly, almost miraculously, he heard the clatter of hooves from beneath. A rider, wrapped in a bright yellow slicker, water pouring from his wide brimmed hat, was reining in below.

"Ho! Up here!" shouted Art.

A wave of relief washed over him as Art saw that the figure below was Alex. He leapt from the saddle and snatched up a rusty, U-shaped chunk of metal that lay discarded near the tracks. With practised hands he fastened the steel to the end of his lariat. Silently signalling Art to stand clear, he swung the rope in a wide, whirling loop and tossed the weight up and through the doorway. Art tied the rope to a beam and without hesitation stepped from the opening and scrambled frantically down the wall.

"How did you know?" asked Art breathlessly.

"Saw the smoke," came the *Stranger's* laconic reply, and the two men watched as the doorway was consumed by the now rampant blaze.

THE SPIDER ON THE HARROP FERRY

It's been over five years now and I've tried to convince myself that it never happened. But I know it did. And I need to talk about it. Please don't think that I'm crazy, because I am not. I know what I saw, and this is what I saw.

I don't want to tell you who I am but I used to live in Harrop, in a house whose balcony on the top floor had a great view of the Harrop Ferry for about half its trip across the West Arm. After that it disappeared behind the big cottonwoods and the bend in the lake for the final two minutes of its journey. I could even check to see when the ferry was leaving the other side, throw on my daypack, say goodbye to my Mom and, if I walked fast, get to the ferry on the Harrop side just as it was ready to leave.

I did that most days because I always walked to school at Redfish just five minutes from the ferry on the other side. I knew that ferry as well as anyone, and I loved it. I loved meeting my friends at the ferry. I loved the sound of the ramps hitting the pavement when the ferry landed, even if my Dad hated it and woke up at night when they made an especially loud noise. I loved playing the jumping game back and forth between the two big concrete blocks that held the ferry's cables. I even loved those black, greasy poles by the ramps with those piston things that let the ramps down. But I never touched them.

It was that summer, five years ago, that I lost my love for the Harrop Ferry. The love wasn't replaced by hate, it was replaced by fear. It was fear mixed with a fascination that started in the spring and took hold of me and wouldn't let go until that fall.

It all started when a bunch of us were watching spiders in their webs on the ferry's railings. We always did that. Some kids were scared of them and wouldn't get close but I always watched them. There were lots of them and many of them got pretty big because there was always a lot of food for them with the ferry going back and forth over the lake. There were always lots of flies and bugs over the water. I even saw grown-ups looking at them and talking about them. This one day we were on our way to school in the spring and a few of us were looking at egg sacks that were tucked up under the top plate of the railing. You had to lean over to see them or squat down and look up underneath. Some of the egg sacks were huge and you could see that there were hundreds of eggs in them. It was no wonder there were always lots of spiders on the ferry.

We only had about four minutes to get across so we were all running around trying to find the biggest egg sack and get the others to come and look. I found one under the railing on the end of the ferry, not the side. It was on the Harrop end of the ferry right near one of those greasy black poles. It wasn't the biggest one anybody had found but it looked different than the rest and for some reason I didn't call anyone over to look at it. The ferry landed on the Redfish side and we all took off up the hill and down Pipper's Lane to the school. I forgot all about the egg sack and didn't look at it for days. When I finally did it looked exactly the same as it had a few days earlier.

The weather got warmer and we started to see changes in the spiders' egg sacks. We were even there to watch a couple of them hatch. I still didn't show anyone else the one I had spotted and I don't know why. I kept an eye on it and over a couple of weeks noticed that it just wasn't changing like the rest of them. But I did finally notice what was different about it. It took me a while to see it but then I finally realized that it wasn't a whole bunch of eggs like all the others. It was a single egg. It was all wrapped up in that sticky web stuff and tucked up tight under the railing like the others, but I never saw a spider near it. And it never changed.

All the others had hatched. There were spiders everywhere, just like last year and the year before. I don't know where they all went because thousands must have hatched out. I guess some of them got eaten or fell into the water or got run over by cars. Every time I was on the ferry I would check "my" spider egg. To this day I still don't know why but I never showed it to anyone and I never made a big deal of looking at it when others were around.

The school year finished and I wasn't on the ferry nearly as much. But I'd still go and look once in a while. I'd get out of the car if we were going to Nelson or Balfour and I'd check on it. Right through to the end of July I watched it and during that whole time it didn't change. I started to get a little sad about it because I thought it must have died before it could hatch. It was about the size of my little fingernail and I thought that surely if it were getting ready to hatch it must swell up first or change in some way. But it always looked the same.

It was about the middle of August that summer and I hadn't been on the ferry in about a week. I had the urge to go and look at the egg sack so I told my Mom I was going to go and ride back and forth on the ferry a few times to cool off in the breeze out over the water. That was okay with her.

I was shocked to see the egg sack gone. Then I saw some scraps of web stuff and what must have been the casing of that egg. I didn't mind that I had missed the hatching. I hadn't expected to see it anyway. But I really did want to see the spider that came out of it and I couldn't see it anywhere. I must have ridden across and back five times and I checked under every railing and looked up and down the posts and the cables for the ramps. I even checked in the little waiting room that I hardly ever went into.

I went back the next day and leaned with my back in the corner where the end railing met the side railing and watched. I pretended I was just out there enjoying the weather but I was watching the whole area where the egg had been. I waved at a few people I knew who drove on and even hung out for a few minutes with a couple of friends who were on their way to the hot springs. But I always went back to my corner and watched.

Then I saw it. It looked just like any of the other spiders on the ferry, only bigger. And it had only hatched a few days ago. I saw it crawl in under the ramps after the cars got on. I couldn't see where it went but it was pretty close to the water before it crawled in under the ferry somewhere. I remembered my Dad telling me about the big hollow spaces under the car deck of the ferry. He had seen the ferry in for repairs when it was in the drydock at Sunshine Bay. That was probably where the spider was hiding. There must have been a hole somewhere.

I saw it a few more times in the next week and it was bigger every time I saw it. It was probably about the size of the palm of my hand by that time. I could never quite see where it crawled in. It was down in under the ramp somewhere and I couldn't lean far enough over the railing to see. The ferry operator even yelled at me once over the loudspeaker to get off the railing. I was so embarrassed because he even knew my name. So I just stood leaning in my corner hoping to see the big spider.

I was starting to be afraid of it but I needed to look at it whenever I could. My family must have thought I was crazy spending so much time on the ferry but my Dad said it was better than watching TV. I think now, looking back on it, that the spider knew I was watching it. I don't know why I think that, it's just a feeling I have. It never looked at me or made any sign that it knew I was there but it seemed to become less shy when I was around. If anybody was with me I never saw it, which suited me just fine because I didn't want to share it with anyone.

It must have been eating a lot of bugs because it just kept getting bigger. By the end of August it was easily as big as both my fists put together. It seemed to know when it was safest to come out because that was usually when the ferry was facing away from Harrop heading to the Redfish side. The people in the cars were all looking in that direction. So was the ferry operator. It was right at a time like that when I saw something that really made me scared.

The ferry was approaching land, when the operator really has to pay attention. Everybody was in their cars; a few had already started their engines.

The spider had climbed up the greasy black post and was right up at the top. I forgot to tell you, one of the other things I really liked to do was to watch the osprey hunting for fish. If you were lucky you could even see them hit the water and come out again with a fish in their claws. Well that had just happened and I was torn between watching the osprey with its fish or watching the spider. Then, for some reason, the osprey lost its fish. He must not have had a good enough grip and the fish must have been struggling like crazy. The fish fell.

The spider must have been watching the osprey fly by. When it saw the fish falling towards the water, and I swear to God this really happened, that spider hooked a web to the top of that post and it swung out over the ferry's ramp and then back out over the water. Its timing was perfect. I couldn't believe it but I had just seen it with my own eyes. At the end of its swinging arc the spider grabbed hold of that fish, it must have been eight or ten inches long, and started to swing back. It let out more line as it was swinging back and smashed into the side of the ramp. The spider wasn't hurt and it didn't let go of the fish. I watched stunned as the spider dragged the fish in under the ramp and disappeared under the ferry.

I didn't see the spider for a few days after that. Eating that fish must have triggered something in the spider because it changed. A week later I saw the spider again hauling a fish underneath the ferry. There was no osprey in sight and the spider was wet. You sometimes see spiders swimming if they fall into water but this one was wet on its back. It had been underwater. Twice more in September I saw that spider with a fish, each time a bigger fish. That was when I stopped walking onto the ferry.

This is why I ask you not to think I'm crazy: the spider was the size of a cat. Even if we went onto the ferry in the car I wouldn't get out. My parents thought it was odd but I just pretended that nothing was wrong and they soon forgot about it.

I started watching the ferry from our balcony. I would wait for it to appear from behind the cottonwoods then I'd train my binoculars on the Harrop end of the ferry as it headed across. It was a warm fall. Three more times in September and October I saw the spider with a fish but it must surely have caught more while I wasn't watching. It appeared to be about the size of our chocolate lab.

Then one night our neighbour's cat went missing. They put up posters the next day at the ferry bulletin board. I heard that some people up on Lewis Road in Harrop had seen a cougar so everybody figured that's probably where the cat went. Then some people over on Erindale Road lost their dog.

Somebody called the Conservation Officer and they hired that guy with the bloodhounds to track the cougar. They shot it. Everybody thought that would be the end of it but a few more cats and another dog, one of those big German shepherds from that man who has so many, went missing in Harrop.

    I was really scared by this time but did my best not to show it. I snuck out onto the balcony one night with the binoculars. The balcony was off our spare bedroom so nobody knew I went out there. It was a full moon near the end of October. I had always heard that deer and elk could swim across a lake. There was even a story going around that the ferry operator had watched a moose swim across the West Arm just upstream from the ferry. But I was still surprised to see a deer go into the water that night on the other side, just down from the ferry. I saw the deer go in and start swimming across to Harrop just as the ferry came out from behind the cottonwoods. My heart was beating like mad. The current carried the deer maybe fifty or a hundred feet downstream so I wasn't worried about it. Then I saw the shape in the water swim out from under the ferry ramp. It swam fast, riding the current, angling back towards Harrop, heading straight for the deer that didn't know it was coming.

    I couldn't see everything that happened because they went underwater. By that time the current had carried them right down in front of our house. I could see movement in the water in the light of the full moon. I could tell that the deer wasn't struggling. I watched in horror and fascination as the spider dragged the dead deer into the shallow water. It was so close I didn't need to and didn't want to use the binoculars. I expected to see the deer hauled up onto the shore and devoured before my eyes, but without hesitation the spider turned while the deer was still floating in the shallow water and began making its way along the shore towards the ferry. It soon disappeared around the bend but my imagination saw the rest. The spider would not eat its prey on land. Its home and its world was the underbelly of the Harrop Ferry. It would drag that beast all the way, swimming with it around the docks that were between our house and the ferry. It would wait in the shadows of the last dock, just metres from the ferry, and when the ramp was up and the operator had turned to face the far shore, it would swim with four or five of its giant hairy legs, the rest holding the deer and reach the ferry before it came out from the cottonwoods.

    I was wrong. It reached the ferry while I was staring at the spot I knew so well, where I had seen my beloved little ferry so often appear with its tattered British Columbia flag flapping wildly in the wind. I saw the spider drag the deer up under the ramp. What great gaping hole was there up above the waterline under that boat that would allow the spider to drag its prey into its lair? Or did it rips the deer's limbs off one at a time and bring all the pieces in before the ferry returned to Harrop? I went back to my own room but didn't sleep that night.

There was a hard frost in early November. I thought about the spider and wondered if it could survive a winter. Could it live on fish it caught in the dead of the night when no one saw? My question was answered a week later in a way I never could have imagined. I recalled my awe and astonishment as I remembered the night I watched the deer enter the water in the light of the full moon. It was another cloudless night and I was restless. I hadn't been sleeping well at all lately and I snuck over to the spare bedroom with the binoculars and out onto the balcony. The cold cedar boards under my bare feet stung as I gazed out over the lake. I scanned the far side, standing first on one foot, then the other, trying to warm the cold foot by placing it on top of the other I was standing on.

What I had felt at seeing the deer a week before was like nothing compared to the shock of what I was now looking at. I had only ever seen one bear in my whole life and that was from the car. And it was a black bear. I could tell by the size and by the great hump on its back that the bear entering the water on the beach across the lake was a grizzly. I had seen many pictures and we had just learned about how bears return to their same hibernating spot each winter. I figured that bear must have been heading to its den somewhere in the mountains up behind us, towards Mill Lake.

The grizzly was a very strong swimmer. He must not have wanted to be carried too far downstream by the current so he was angling slightly upstream with the result being that he was swimming straight across. I didn't want to look upstream to the bend in the lake for fear of what I might see. I had heard the ramp slam onto the pavement a few minutes earlier so I knew that the ferry was heading back to the other side. I didn't want to look but I had to. The shape I saw heading towards the bear shocked me because I thought it was the bear itself. I soon realized that the spider with its heavy body and its huge hairy legs and its awesome mouth parts was the same size as the grizzly. I wondered at how many fish and perhaps what else it had eaten since that terrible night with the deer.

The bear saw the spider coming. I expected it to turn and swim downstream to the shore and move on its powerful legs across the beach, through the trees and over the tracks and disappear into the mountains. But it turned and swam toward its attacker. The half moon light was pale but I could see the water churning as they grappled with each other. Both were hairy, both were dark and I could never quite tell which beast was on the water and which was submerged by the awesome strength of the other. There was an incredible beauty to the movement, like two great dancers holding each other tightly while rolling elegantly in the cold current of Kootenay Lake. But this was no dance and these were no loving embraces.

They were straight in front of our house now. I noticed how cold my feet were. I made no move to warm them. My whole body was cold but I knew that the violent shivering that shook the binoculars in my hands was from more than the cold. I truly didn't know how the fight would turn out. Then I saw a great black shape dragging itself up onto our beach. I glanced back out onto the water and saw another drifting slowly with the current. It was still. I looked again in horror at that spot on the beach where I had played so often.

The beast lay for a minute or two then shook the water from the fur of its great black head. It rose slowly onto all four legs and started walking down the beach away from my house. I could tell that it was limping badly with one of its front legs and that it was actually dragging a back leg. It disappeared into the trees. I've always wondered if that bear ever made it to its den to hibernate or if it found a quiet spot in the forest to lick its wounds and perhaps die.

The spider? I'm sure the bottom feeders feasted on that great black carcass as it hung up somewhere in the rocky depths of the West Arm. I only know that I want to be there next time the Harrop Ferry goes to the drydock for repairs. I want to see the bones.

ZEUS AND JUPITER FILL THEIR LUNGS—A NEW LOOK AT THE BEAUFORT WIND SPEED SCALE

Do you remember the fable of the Sun and the Wind? It is the tale of a great competition between two great powers that live in the sky above our Earth. Well, after I remind you of that contest, I will tell you of another between two even greater powers who live all around and in and below our world, and maybe even in us people down here on Earth. I am talking about the great Greek god Zeus and his equal the Roman god Jupiter.

You'll remember how once, long ago, the Sun and the Wind were high in the sky looking down upon the Earth. Being a little bored they were looking for something exciting to do. The Sun then saw a traveler making his way on foot across a great plain. The Sun called to the Wind to look at the man walking across the lonely land. The Wind looked down and saw the man with coat buttoned up tight to his throat and his hand in his pockets, for it was a cold day. The Wind said to the Sun: "Let's have a little fun with that fellow and see if we can take off his coat." The Sun agreed to the contest and told the Wind to go first.

The Wind swooped down from the sky and began to tug at the man's hat. The man pulled his hat down tighter over his ears and kept walking. The Wind then swirled around the man's feet and up his legs and under his coat. The man wrapped his arms around himself and shivered at the sudden breeze that so suddenly blew around him. The wind blew stronger and made the man's coattails flap around his legs. He wrapped his arms even tighter and leaned into the wind that blew hard in his face. The Wind became angry at the man and blew harder, getting up his sleeves, through his buttonholes and down the back of his neck. The harder the Wind blew, the colder the man became and the harder he held his arms tight. Try as he might the Wind could not blow the coat off the man.

The Sun smiled warmly at the Wind and asked him to move aside, for it was now the Sun's turn. The man's arms dropped to his sides as the wind left him and raged back into the sky to watch from above. The man looked all about wondering where that sudden strong Wind had gone. He felt the Sun shine down on him and was happy that the chilling Wind was no longer bothering him. The Sun shone even stronger and its warmth went into the man making him forget all about the chill he had just had from the Wind. Soon the man took his hat off as the Sun beat down upon his head and back. The Sun made the man's shoulders very warm and he soon undid the top button of his coat. Before long he had opened the second and the third buttons and he could feel prickly heat on his back and arms. Without a thought suddenly all the buttons were open and the man was walking with his coat flapping about him as he tried to cool himself. The Wind watched as the man finally took his coat off and carried it folded up ever his arm. It may have taken him a little longer but the Sun had won the contest.

You may have heard of the ancient Greeks and Romans who lived thousands of years ago. They believed that there were gods who controlled the sun and the stars and the winds and the ocean and the seasons and the plants and animals. The stories of the Greek and Roman gods are many and the most exciting stories are about the chief gods, the ones who controlled all the rest. The Greeks called their main god Zeus, while the chief god of the ancient Romans was Jupiter.

Not all of the stories of the gods are written down in books. In fact, the Romans and the Greeks didn't even know that sometimes their gods got together to talk, or argue or sometimes, like in this story, have contests. Just like the Sun and the Wind story, there was also a time when Zeus and Jupiter were cruising around in the sky above the Earth, looking down to see if there was any mischief they could make. Everything was calm; in fact it was so calm that that they looked at the day below them and both remarked on how boring the world looked to them.

Jupiter sailed out over the ocean and saw the calm, smooth water below him. If he had been visible, which he wasn't, he would have shown up in the surface of the ocean, which was a still as glass and reflected the blue sky and few clouds like a perfect mirror.

Zeus was hovering over a great forest on one of the continents that had very few people on it. The day was so calm that not a leaf rustled and the smoke from the one little campfire that he saw went straight up into the sky without bending or drifting.

"What a dull, boring day!" Zeus and Jupiter said to each other as they looked down upon the land and the sea. It is not clear who had the idea first but it was soon clear to both of them that if they were going to have any fun, they were going to have to stir things up a bit. So Jupiter said to Zeus: "You take the land and I'll take the sea and we'll see who can blow the hardest and make our wind felt down there on the Earth."

A challenge was a challenge and Zeus had never backed down from a challenge. He knew that he and Jupiter were probably about exactly equal in strength but he was always willing to see who was stronger, smarter, faster, better or trickier at anything that could be tested with a contest.

They decided to have a close look at the land and ocean to make sure they were starting from the same level and that the contest was fair. Fairness was something the gods always argued about. So they both declared that the air was "calm." Jupiter reported that the sea was as smooth as a mirror while Zeus said that the leaves were silent and the smoke from the fire was rising absolutely vertically. The two gods agreed to start out small and work their way up to great, billowing, blustering, blowing breaths and find out fairly who had the strongest lungs.

With just a puff of his cheeks, Jupiter sent a "light air" out over the ocean. If we were to put it into today's language that little puff travelled across the water at about two to five kilometres per hour, or about the speed of a child walking somewhere in no hurry at all. The air from Jupiter's cheeks glided across the water stirring up the surface so it looked like the scales of a fish. But the tiny waves did not break or make a foamy crest.

Zeus was watching carefully and puffed his cheeks up the same as Jupiter and sent his "light air" out over the forested land. It was the same speed as Jupiter's first wind and did not even rustle the leaves but it did send that little column of smoke drifting slowly downwind in the direction that Zeus had blown. Before Jupiter could blow again Zeus inhaled a small breath and sent it out over the forest. The little wind that followed was called a "light breeze" and it set the leaves in the trees to rustle until Zeus finished his breath. The smoke blew away.

Jupiter sent his own "light breeze" out over the ocean. It was the same speed that Zeus had created, what we would call six to eleven kilometres per hour, like a child running slowly, but still in no real hurry. The scale-like movement of the water changed to wavelets with glassy crests but not yet breaking. Jupiter had seen how Zeus hurried with his last turn so he did the same. He took a deeper breath than last time and sent it out over the sea. The light breeze changed to a "gentle breeze" which raced across the water faster than most children can run for long, twelve to eighteen kilometres per hour. The wavelets changed to large wavelets, some of them breaking and making whitecaps.

Zeus carefully filled his Greek lungs with the same amount of air as his Roman friend had done and sent his own "gentle breeze" into the forest. The leaves rustled loudly, fluttering back and forth as the godly wind passed over them. But the branches they hung from were still. Jupiter was watching carefully and sent his next breath out over the water, as Zeus was finishing his last. The wavelets changed to small waves, which were much longer and many of them broke, sending whitecaps into the sea. This "moderate breeze" was stirring the ocean.

Zeus copied Jupiter exactly. Now not only the leaves were rustling but also the branches were swaying in the breath of the Greek god. Maybe a very fast child could run as fast as that wind which we would measure at nineteen to thirty kilometres per hour.

Now there was no more waiting for each other to take their turns. Zeus and Jupiter took a breath and blew out strongly over land and sea. Today we see cars in a town travelling thirty-one to thirty-nine kilometres per hour, the same speed as the "fresh breeze" the two gods had made. Small trees were swaying in the wind. Every leaf was fluttering wildly. Waves on the ocean were high and long, most of them crashing with many of the whitecaps being blown off as foamy spray.

Again the two gods inhaled and blew even harder out over forest and ocean. Faster than the fastest man the "strong breeze" was bending the thick branches of the great fir trees of the forest. Whitecaps were now breaking off every wave sending spray from wave to wave. Jupiter and Zeus knew nothing of the words we use today but the force from their lungs was sending the wind up to forty to fifty kilometres per hour.

Their next breathy blast was "near gale" force. On land whole trees were now in motion, bending and swaying but still staying strong in the face of the wind. On the sea the waves were now turning to swells, heaping up on each other, breaking into great foamy streaks blown out in front of Jupiter's breath. We on Earth today would call the speed fifty-one to sixty-one kilometres per hour.

Now the challenge between the two gods was getting serious. Without pause they both filled their lungs and blew hard, Jupiter over the ocean, Zeus over the forest. This was more than just a wind; this was a "gale." Trees were whipping violently about with many small branches and twigs snapping off in the wind. Up to seventy-four kilometres per hour, the gale raised higher, longer waves that crested and broke into spindrift, a frothy foam that blew off the breaking waves and streaked in wild lines across the heaving ocean.

Another deep breath, another great exhalation of wind as the two gods blew over land and sea. Great gusts of up to eighty-seven kilometres per hour, called a "strong gale" bent trees almost to the breaking point. Many large branches could not withstand the force and snapped off to be blown far from the mother tree. Even the houses of the people who lived near the forest were beginning to suffer from the force of the strong gale as it lifted loose shingles and rattled windows. The wind of Jupiter had raised high waves, which turned into rolling seas that sent dense streaks of foam across the water. If any ships were in the area their sails would be flapping violently, the smallest of them tearing off completely and the crew could not see more than three ship lengths through the foam beyond the bow.

Is there anything greater than a strong gale which some call a "severe gale"? Yes, there is the "storm" which can reach speeds of up to one hundred two kilometres per hour. Can you imagine a wind travelling at the speed of a car on the freeway? Well the storm is that fast and it is not yet the fastest of the winds. The two gods called upon their beyond human strength and blew storm force winds across land and sea. Windows broke in houses. Trees fell, the weakest and smallest giving way while the larger, stronger stood and faced the awesome blast. Very high waves crested and curled with great overhanging caps that blew dense foam across the water creating white patches like fields of snow. May all the gods help the poor sailors who may have been out in that storm, for though they may have survived, they would have seen very little beyond their bow and their sails would have been in tatters.

Zeus and Jupiter rested a moment to gather their strength and prepare for the next blast of force upon land and ocean. Together they filled their lungs and held, took in even more of the world's air and pushed with the strength of ancient gods against the Earth. What they caused is called a "violent storm," one hundred seventeen kilometres per hour of destruction, which broke proud trees as old as the gods themselves and lifted roofs off the houses of the poor unsuspecting people who knew nothing of the game the gods were playing outside their doors. The waves on the sea were as high as the great old trees which were crashing to the ground in the forest. Patches of thick, white foam covered the ocean between the towering waves and if sailors were fools enough or unlucky enough to out there, they would have seen nothing beyond the point as far as they could spit.

We've heard now of the stages of wind that Zeus and Jupiter brought upon our Earth. From calm, through light air and the breezes and the gales and the storms, the two gods looked at each other and knew that the contest was soon over for they were reaching even the limits of their awesome, godlike strength. They rested a while, called upon the forces of other, lesser gods to give them more strength. The people of the land found shelter in caves and cellars and the deepest gulleys where the wind never blew. Sailors hurried to harbours, fisherfolk pulled in their nets, dropped anchor behind islands of rock, and the world waited as the two great gods looked at each other from land and sea.

Zeus and Jupiter rested longer, each watching the other for any sign of trickery. The people of land and sea thought that perhaps the unusual storm was over, that perhaps they could come out of their safe places and begin to rebuild their lives. But it is good that they were cautious and that they waited. Both gods inhaled a deep and might breath. So great was the sucking of air that trees fell in the other direction as from the violent storm. They waved their arms about forcing more air into their godly lungs. They grabbed handfuls of air and forced them into their mouths until their bodies swelled. Animals were gasping for breath because there was not enough air left in the world for all the creatures of the Earth.

And the gods blew! Pity the people who may have been out on land or sea! They did not survive that wind. The numbers do not mean much anymore at that speed. The wind may have been one hundred forty-eight kilometres per hour. Or perhaps one hundred eighty-three or over two hundred. Whatever people of today may call it, it was a "hurricane" and it left its mark upon the land and in the hearts and minds of the people. Zeus flattened villages, ripped ancient trees from the ground and tossed them against cliffs to shatter and fall in shame and defeat, even their great roots deep in the Earth unable to hold them fast. Do you want to know the meaning of the word destruction? Look to the damage done by the breath of Zeus upon the forest and the people of the land.

And Jupiter? Ah, Jupiter blew with the strength of a god whose pride was challenged by his oldest sometime friend and rival. Jupiter released his built up force across the water so that it was impossible to say where the water ended and the air began. The sea was completely white with driving spray. If anybody could be there, which he couldn't, he would not have seen beyond his nose. Waves were crashing in every direction. Great seas washed up onto the land, leveling forests already damaged by the wind of Zeus. Islands were flooded, ships were beached, foam from the frothy sea was driven up into the highlands where mountain goats had their first taste of salt.

And when it was all over? Who won? Jupiter and Zeus were both exhausted. They had both caused hurricane force winds to ravage the land and the sea. They each thought they had outdone the other. They went back to their homes in the skies above Greece and Italy to hurl their thunderbolts down upon the unsuspecting people. But who won the contest? Maybe even with the destruction the gods brought upon the Earth it was the people who won.

We learned to enjoy the calm of a beautiful day when lakes and oceans are a mirror to reflect the sky and the forest is so silent we can hear ourselves think. We learned to enjoy the cooling breeze which blows over us as we are sweating with our work upon the Earth. We learned to stop as the wind blows harder and look up from our labours and listen to the rustling in the leaves or the fluttering of the sails. We learned to find our own strength as we lean into the wind that pushes us and forces us to dig in our feet and push back. We learned to know when our minds must tell us to find a safe harbour or shelter from the storm.

The gods will come again and again and we will not see them as they blow their blustery, pride filled breath upon us and our Earth, but we will use their strength for our purposes, we will harness the power of their games and tame it for us and our children. And when they see that we are using their own strength for us, they will get angry and blow harder, and we will hide until their strength is gone. Then we will come out and we will look around and we will laugh!

WIND CHILL, FROSTBITE AND HYPOTHERMIA

Ugo was a boy from the country of Ecuador in South America. He wasn't sure whether he was really lucky or really unlucky when he thought about the trip he was about to take with his family. His Dad was a meteorologist with the Ecuadorian government and he had to go on a trip to northern Canada to study winter weather in the north. His father tried to get his boss to just let him learn about the weather from books and the Internet but the Chief Meteorologist had told him there is nothing like feeling the weather on your own skin to learn what it is really like.

Because he had to stay up there for three months Ugo's whole family was allowed to go along. That's why Ugo wasn't sure if he was lucky or unlucky. He felt lucky because none of his friends had ever been to Canada at all, let alone to a place with a name as strange sounding as Tuktoyaktuk. He thought maybe he was unlucky because his father had told him that the temperature was minus forty degrees and that there was only about three hours of daylight. Ugo had never been out of Ecuador. He had felt forty degrees many times but that was plus forty! And because he lived near the equator, day and night were always about the same length, all year round.

But Ugo was ready for an adventure. A house was arranged for them to live in although he wasn't so happy that he and his sister Maria would have to share a room. Maria was eight. Ugo was ten. He was happy that he and Maria would be going to school in Tuktoyaktuk, otherwise he would probably be bored if he had to stay home the whole time. He had been learning English in school so he knew he would understand a lot of what was being said in the classroom, even though he knew he'd be shy about trying to talk in English. His Dad spoke English well and was even going to be spending time in his school.

Ugo remembered the time he had asked his Dad what a meteorologist was. His Dad had laughed because Ugo thought it was somebody who studied meteors, but he explained that it was a person who studied the weather. His Dad had studied it in English so he would be able to talk to the kids about the winter weather when he came into the school as part of his work.

The flight was long and boring, but after many stops they finally arrived in Tuk. Ugo was glad that the nickname of Tuktoyaktuk was Tuk so he didn't always have to say such a hard to pronounce name. He had learned on the

Internet that the name Tuktoyaktuk was the English pronunciation of an Inuvialuit name meaning, "resembles a caribou." Apparently there were reefs in the Artic Ocean off Tuk that looked like a caribou when the water was out at low tide.

It was dark when they arrived and Ugo and Maria went right to bed. It was dark when they got up, too. Ugo had heard that in the summer the far north was called the land of the midnight sun, but he was here in the dead of winter. He knew that they were not all that far from the North Pole so he figured the South Pole must be the land of the midnight sun at this time of year. They had a few days before they went to school so they could at least get used to the place.

The weather was not as cold as Ugo thought it was going to be. It was only minus twenty. He went outside with his sister and his Dad. "Minus twenty doesn't even seem all that cold," Ugo said to his Dad. They were standing in the yard behind the house. They were dressed in many layers of clothes. Dad said: "That's because there is no wind here, Ugo. If we walk around to the front of the house, you'll feel the difference when we are standing in the wind."

They walked around the corner of the house and a breeze about fifteen kilometres per hour hit them in the face. Both of them automatically pulled their coats tighter around them and covered the exposed skin on their faces. "Wow, that's a lot colder in the wind," Ugo said. Dad, who had just been reading about temperature and wind said: "Actually it's not colder, Ugo. It just feels colder. That's what we call the Wind Chill Factor." Ugo argued that if it feels colder then it is colder. The wind felt like it was biting the skin on his face.

His Dad then explained to him what "wind chill" meant. "Okay, it's minus twenty out here. That's the temperature. There is a wind blowing at about fifteen kilometres per hour. Meteorologists," and he pointed at himself, "have a way of figuring out how to put temperature and wind together to get the wind chill factor. So with a fifteen kilometer per hour wind at minus twenty, that makes it feel like minus twenty-nine."

Ugo said: "But if it feels like minus twenty-nine, then it is minus twenty-nine." His Dad said: "Let me try to explain it to you in another way. When you are standing in a calm place you have an envelope of air around you that warms up because you are standing there. If a wind blows onto you it blows away that air around you. But because you are a warm object standing there you will try to keep reheating that envelope of air around you. And the wind will keep blowing it away. That's why it feels colder than it really is. The wind is actually sucking the heat out of you and making you cool down faster than if there were no wind."

"Let's do a little experiment," his Dad said.

"Why don't we wait until you visit the school next week," Ugo said. "Then you can do the experiment with everyone." His Dad agreed.

It turned into a couple of weeks before Ugo's Dad came into the classroom but that gave Maria and Ugo time to get settled in and get to know everybody, which was easy because it was a small school.

A cold snap had hit Tuk and it was now minus thirty degrees outside. Ugo and Maria had learned quickly to dress for the weather. Ugo had learned the hard way. He had gone out one day without mittens. He didn't get frostbite but it gave him a good taste of what frostbite could be like. His fingers were so cold he could not move them and when he did get back inside they hurt like crazy when they finally warmed up. His Dad had said he'd give the kids a lesson about frostbite at school when he came to talk about weather.

Well, now was that time and an experiment about wind chill was all set up to show the mixed class of grade three, four and five students. Mr. Ramos (Ugo still called him Dad) had brought six portable thermometers. The permanent one on the side of the school that the class could see from the window read minus thirty. All the thermometers in the classroom read plus twenty degrees. Everybody was dressed to go outside. One group brought a thermometer out behind the school where it was sheltered and the wind was calm. The other group, Ugo's group, brought a thermometer out the front door where the wind was blowing at about twenty kilometres per hour. Each group had a stopwatch. Somebody held the thermometer at the top so the heat from the person's hand would not affect the thermometer. One was in calm air, the other in the wind. The two groups timed how long it took for the temperature to fall to minus thirty. The group on the windy side of the school was back in the classroom long before the others. Ugo was starting to understand what his father had meant by wind chill.

Mr. Ramos explained what had happened with the thermometers. "What you observed out there is called the 'wind chill factor.' The temperature is minus thirty. The wind is twenty kilometres per hour. There's some tricky math you do with those two numbers which gives you the 'wind chill temperature.' At this temperature and wind speed the wind chill temperature is minus forty, or actually minus forty-point-one if you want to be exact. But you'll notice that even on the windy side of the school, with the wind chill temperature of minus forty, the temperature on the thermometer did not go below minus thirty. It just dropped to minus thirty a lot faster than on the windstill side of the school.

"So when you are out in that wind, the temperature is not really at minus forty on a thermometer. It just feels like minus forty. And just like the thermometers we observed, you, too, will cool down a lot faster in the wind than out of the wind. So wind chill is more about how the temperature feels than what it actually is."

Ugo and the rest of the kids in the class thought they were starting to understand it. Mr. Ramos got the kids to gather around a computer. He showed them a wind chill calculator on a weather website. They took turns typing in temperature and wind speed then clicking on 'calculate.' Minus thirty with a twenty-five kilometre per hour wind became a minus forty-four wind chill temperature. Mr. Ramos asked how cold it can get in Tuktoyaktuk and was told that it usually get down to minus forty. The kids didn't know how strong the wind could get but the teacher said they often had forty kilometre per hour winds. One of the kids punched in the numbers, clicked on calculate and found the wind chill temperature of less than minus sixty.

One boy said that he had heard his Dad talk about the antifreeze in his truck. His Dad had heard that the wind chill temperature was going down to minus fifty-five. He said that the antifreeze in his truck would only work down to minus forty. Mr. Ramos smiled and said: "that is exactly what we are talking about here. Tell your Dad that the antifreeze will be all right. It will not freeze with that wind chill temperature. The actual temperature will not go below minus forty. His truck will just cool down a lot faster to reach minus forty but will not get colder, even if the wind keeps blowing or gets stronger and drives the wind chill temperature down to minus sixty."

Ugo reminded his Dad that he was going to tell them about frostbite. Mr. Ramos asked the class who knew what frostbite was. Everybody except Maria and Ugo knew what it was. None of them had ever had it but some had seen people who had had it.

"I'm not a doctor, I'm a meteorologist but I have studied it quite carefully and know a lot about it. Do you really want to hear what frostbite can do to a person? Some of the details are not very pretty." Everybody wanted to hear all the details.

Mr. Ramos asked if anybody had ever seen ice. They all laughed saying of course they had. So he asked if they understood what it meant when water froze. Again they all laughed. They live in Tuk where everything around them was almost always frozen. "Well," said Mr. Ramos, "frostbite is actually when part of a person freezes. The deeper the freezing, the more dangerous it is to the person. If the freezing is just the very outer layer of skin, then the person will recover from it. But it can get pretty nasty. It happens mostly on the fingers, toes, cheeks, ears and even the nose. And it can happen quickly before you really notice it." Mr. Ramos described how the skin could turn white and hard and if the freezing went deeper it could turn purple or even black. The children were silent as he talked about people losing fingers and toes and ears or getting deep damage on cheeks and other exposed body parts. Ugo and Maria were amazed that such a thing could happen but some of the kids from Tuk just nodded and said they knew people with bad scars or missing fingers from frostbite.

"And it can happen even faster in the wind," Mr. Ramos said, reminding them about the wind chill factor. They all exchanged stories about family members or friends who had had frostbite and Ugo and Maria gained a whole new respect for the cold and what the people of the far north had to deal with most of the year.

They learned that there was a stage of frostbite that didn't do any real damage and that most of them had probably had. It was called frostnip. That was when your hands or feet got so cold that they ached like crazy when they warmed up. Almost everybody, even Ugo, said that they had had frostnip.

There's one more thing I need to talk about," said Mr. Ramos, "because this is something that can even kill you if you are not careful. And this one, too, is even worse in the wind. Has anybody ever heard the word hypothermia?" Some had, some hadn't. "Remember how I described how the wind blows that envelope of warm air from around you? Well people and animals are always producing more heat from inside. It comes from the food we eat. Imagine the wind blowing so hard that it is blowing away your own body heat faster than your body can produce it. Or imagine being wet and in a cold wind, or falling into icy water. That's when your body temperature can fall faster than your body can replace the lost heat. Your actual body temperature will drop. Hypothermia! Do you hear the word thermia in there? Like in the word thermometer? Well it just means heat. And hypo means under or below or abnormally low. So hypothermia is your body cooling off very fast until your temperature is so low that you'll actually be sick.

"If you have hypothermia your speech will be slurred, your breathing will slow down, your skin will be pale and cold, you'll be unusually tired and you'll probably get the 'umbles.' It's kind of a joke but it is really serious and nothing to laugh about. The 'umbles' are the stumbles, the mumbles, the fumbles and the grumbles. These are all things you will probably do if you have hypothermia."

Mr. Ramos went on to explain what to do if someone has hypothermia, but that is for another story. The best thing to do is avoid hypothermia and if you do feel like you are getting it, get inside and warm up! Same thing for frostbite!

THE FOUR LITTLE WATER DROPLETS

Four tiny water droplets lived together in a castle high in the clouds. They were all sisters and brothers but they were as different as night and day, as black and white, as long and short or as thick and thin.

One brother, the strongest, loved it when the wind whipped through the courtyard of their castle, sending spray and wisps of cloud swirling around their garden. He would rush out and call to the wind, challenging it to do battle with him. The hardest fight made him the happiest of all.

His sister, who was a little older, had her favourite place in the safest corner of the castle. She thought about how nice it would be to live somewhere where the wind never blew and where she could spend her days resting, reading good books, drinking tea with honey and eating as much as she pleased. She put on another sweater as she glanced out the window and saw her brother fly by hanging onto a piece of tattered cloud.

Her older brother joined her at the window and peered out with sad, tired eyes. He was sure the castle would be torn apart by the ferocious wind and he just could not understand his brother battling the buffeting wind and even seeming to enjoy it. What a sad, unhappy world we live in, he thought as he looked out at the fierce grey day.

Cheer up, cried the fourth droplet, their little sister, who could never sit still. She raced from window to window, calling to her battling brother to look out behind. She jumped up and down wishing she was allowed to go out into the storm. She pretended the nearest curtain was a wild, windblown mist trying to take her over the garden wall. She wrestled it to the floor, tumbling backwards as she conquered the curtain that came to the floor with her. She rushed back to the window knowing that the storm would soon be over, her brother would be safe and they could all go back out to play.

Soon the wind did stop and the wild brother stormed into the house. He was tattered and breathing hard and there was a strange gleam in his eyes, but he was very happy. His little sister listened to every word of his story as he told of the battle. His older sister brought him a cup of tea. His brother just shook his head and went to his room.

That afternoon their father, the king, called them all together. He told them that they were to go on a long journey and they were to leave now. He wished them well and assured them that although they would be gone a long time, they would surely come back. Hand in hand they left the courtyard of the cloud castle and walked to the edge of the cloud. They stood looking down into the endless space below them, each droplet full of its own thoughts. One thought of the fun they'd have flying down and of all the adventures that were sure to meet them. Another was sure they'd all be smashed to pieces on a rock. A third thought she would much rather be back home in her warm, safe room with that new book she had just started. Let's go, cried the wild brother as he grabbed the other three and jumped with them off the cloud.

Around and around they flew, falling, falling, falling. They held tight to each other knowing that they wanted to stay together. Soon they landed with a little plop in the middle of a tiny mountain lake. Never before had they seen so much water.

Floating, sinking, swimming and splashing, they felt themselves slowly being pulled to one end of the lake. Oh no, where is it taking us now, said the sad brother. Let's go and find out, said the little sister rising up onto the top of a little wave to try and see further ahead. After me, shouted her wild brother who splashed past her and headed in the direction they were going. Why don't we just stay here, asked the oldest sister. This lake is so nice and calm.

Something stronger than all of them brought them to the end of the lake. They could see a little river rushing out and disappearing around the side of a mountain. Suddenly they were pulled faster and faster. They barely had time to catch hold of each other's hands and soon the lake was behind them.

What great fun, called the happy sister as she leapt from spray to foam. Her raging brother had his back to her and was swimming mightily, trying to go upstream against this force that was pulling him. We're doomed, thought the gloomy brother. Surely something terrible is going to happen to us. The other sister could only look ahead to see if she could see some quiet water where she would finally have her peace.

Down, down, down the rapid river they were carried, each accepting, fighting, complaining about or enjoying the ride to the valley below. The little river flowed into a larger one and right away the four water droplets felt the difference. The oldest was worried about the amazing depth of their new home. The second oldest was simply relieved to slow down a bit, but she was far from content. The two youngest were ready for anything. She was already exploring their new surroundings, the likes of which she had never seen before. He was on the lookout for new challenges and was happy, although he would never admit it, to rest a while from his battle with the torrent. They rarely agreed on anything except that they knew they wanted to stay together.

It was a fascinating, fun and sometimes scary journey through the wide, wide valley. They were pushed by cold currents coming in from a blue, glacial stream. They were pulled to the bottom and dragged across slimy rocks and sunken logs. They were spun around by eddies and whirlpools that had captured sticks and leaves and bits of moss. Once they were sucked into the mouth of a giant river sturgeon and blown out again through his gills before the wild brother even had time to protest.

On the surface, at the bottom, in the middle, on the edges they flowed and flowed, following the irresistible force that moved them ever downstream. Near a shore they flowed into a canal whose sides were lined with giant rocks. The canal wandered past farms and fields and big gardens. They watched as some of the water around them was sucked up and sprayed onto newly planted fields.

Once, near a town that lay by the river's edge, they were pulled into the total darkness of a big pipe. Helplessly they travelled quickly through the big pipe, then got pulled into a smaller one, then a smaller one and even a smaller one, speeding and speeding and holding tightly to each other not knowing where they would end up. Finally they found themselves squirted into a place which they did not understand at all. It was very warm and soapy and they were swished and swirled around by a big yellow dishrag. Over knives and forks and in and out of cups and bowls they spun dizzily, only to be soon sucked down into a gurgling black hole.

Before they knew it they had gone through more pipes and were back in the wide river drifting underneath a train bridge. They flowed and flowed with that slow, lazy river. The banks on either side got farther and farther away as the wide, slow river got even wider and slower. They saw many bridges overhead and what they could see of the land was covered with buildings, big and small. They floated past boats for fishing, boats filled with happy, laughing people and boats that were so long they couldn't see both ends at the same time.

The pulling of the river had always been strong and always forward. It moved them to a place where there was no forward and there were no shores to pass. The pulling was still just as strong but it was no longer just in one direction. Now they went down, up and in great looping circles and spirals that took days and even weeks to complete.

Sometimes they even thought they were lying still, but they knew they were in a great, great water almost as deep and wide as forever, which was alive around them and of which they were a part.

The ocean felt like a home where their long journey had led them. They were happy, peaceful and together. It was a beautiful feeling that all four of them shared, also with the countless other drops around them who carried them and whom they carried. The wild younger brother was as calm as his peace-loving older sister while she felt his excitement to be part of this great ocean. The oldest brother felt no fear in exploring with his little sister the deepest, darkest, coldest places or the bright, life-filled water up near the air. They felt at home and it was very good.

Time meant nothing to them. They were in the ocean and the ocean was in them. Movement, flowing, drifting, ocean, home, peace, home, moving, home, ocean.

A time came when they felt a new kind of pulling. They were near the air, surrounded by warmth and light. This new kind of pulling was different than the drifting which had been their life in the ocean. It was a very warm pulling which grew brighter and brought them so close to the air that only their backs were in the warm mother of the ocean beneath them and they touched the warm air above them with their faces. The warm air caressing their bodies awakened in them the feeling of another home which was outside the ocean.

The warm feeling grew warmer and they drifted toward it with no fear and no struggle. The warm air caressed them down their sides and across their backs and lifted them from the mother who had been their home.

Like the current that carried them to the ocean, waves of warm light stroked their bodies and drew them upward toward the bright, shining father who called their names. They listened, remembering the castle that had once been their home. A longing for the great mother beneath them filled their hearts, but they did not look back. They knew they would some day return to her. They knew as surely as they remembered the day their father told them they would return to him some day.

RAVENSHADOW

The sweatband around my forehead is near saturation. My eyes follow carefully the strokes of the hoe inches from my toes. My arms and legs and back ache from the work, the slight bending, the row after row after row. I know I will go on until the last row is done. I know my eyes will not see the hills around me, which I know so well, for at least two hours more. I know I will not look up at the sun which is beating harshly upon my bare back. I will finish my work. I know me. I revel in my human will to ignore the discomfort, to block out the beauty around me, to singlemindedly focus on that which I have set out to do. The hoe cleaves the earth before me. I deftly sever lambsquarters, clover, dandelion and chop them swiftly into the newly softened soil around each plant. The space to the next plant is quickly freed of weeds. The path before me lies littered with the fallen victims of my hoe as I step forward and feel them under my bare feet. I feel the sun, hear the slight breeze in the nearby orchard, smell the dust, the plants, my own sweat. But I will finish. These messages brought to me will not distract me. I will not look up. I will finish. I anticipate the moment when the last weed falls, the last row is complete. I anticipate but I do not yet try to imagine my back straightening, my hands opening, my eyes scanning, the quick glance at the sun to tell me within ten minutes the time near midday. I know already how the water in the nearby stream will feel around my ankles, but I don't dwell there. My eyes follow carefully the strokes of the hoe. I feel the tickling of skin stretching under dried sweat. The sun on my back is a hot blanket. The wind has died. It is all so perfect: the strokes of my hoe are expert, the weeds fall where they must, my resolve is firm. My eyes will not waver.

It is like ice on my back. How long is a moment? That's how long it was there. A moment of ice, a coolness that touched my back, crept under the blanket, then was gone. My mind held that moment, felt it again and again and again all in the space of time it took to close my eyes for a blink. Not close and open, just close. In the time it took for them to open again, I knew, yet my mind re-examined the ice, turned it over and over to see if, no to allow for the hope that it wasn't what I already knew it was. My lashes lifted and my mind asked beseechingly, was that an eagle, an osprey, perhaps even a great blue heron? Them I could have resisted. But I knew already it was the raven. Who else could cast a shadow that cold? Who else would even try to touch me with his shadow, if try he did? I knew it was his will that touched my back with that icy stroke. My eyes were wide open now from that blink.

My hoe hesitated in mid-stroke. I fought to pull it down, to hack into the base of the tiny mullein in my path. But I knew he'd be looking to see if I would look up. Eagle, osprey would have been chance, they'd have flown on uninterested in me, I'd have struck that mullein, watched it fall. My hoe faltered, my head turned. I saw his head turn back to the direction of his flight just as I looked at him.

He knew. I watched him for another second. I heard him make a sound that was new to me. I knew his caws and chortles, his anger, his gloating, his hunger, even his mating sounds. But this was different. This was for me, to me. The ice returned to my back with that new sound. Damn him! He knew that I knew he knew.

SOSTRIS AND HIS GODS

A Picture of Life in Ancient Egypt

Sostris knew every square inch of his land. That it was *his* land did not occur to him, but in practice and in fact the land belonged to him much more than to the king he served but never saw. Or better, he belonged to the land.

As a child he had played with the stones and brown earth of which the land was made. He had played with the silt that covered the land after the yearly flood, tracing with a stick a miniature network of canals like that which his father maintained to irrigate the land. When he was too old to play he had gone with his father and Renn, the servant, into the canals, wading ankle-deep in the sludge, gathering it in wooden basins to distribute on the fields and free the waterways.

He worked with hoe and spade, months rolling into years, cultivating, planting, harvesting. He sat on the earth to eat his simple mid-day meal, the sun-browned skin of his bare, thin legs blending with the colour of the dirt.

He gathered reeds from the river marsh to mend the thatch roof. He carried countless jugs of water for use in the house, his leathery bare feet sure on the uneven path. He planted and tended the vegetable garden, the barley, the corn, learning their seasons and their needs. He walked endless hours behind the crude, ox-drawn plough. He formed clay tiles with his hands, milled the corn, picked the grapes and did a hundred other tasks that his parents and his grandparents and a forgotten number of generations before them had done. He was born on this land and would die on this land.

He was this land.

For Sostris life meant work. From earliest childhood he was told of his duty: service to the gods. The king who lived in the great palace in the city was a direct descendant of the sun god Re, and commanded worship and material production from all his subjects. Sostris had gone many times with his father to the village to pay the taxes levied by the king. Great baskets of barley and flax, clay jugs of wine and offerings of choice meats and fruits were given to the king as tribute to the gods.

The land was fertile, renewed each year by the silt-carrying flood. The king's engineers oversaw the irrigation systems, assuring maximum yield from the valley farmland. On expanses of pasture among the cultivated fields grazed herds of cattle, goats, sheep and donkeys. A large portion of the products obtained from these animals went to the king; the farmers were permitted to keep enough for a modest existence.

As a youth Sostris was fortunate to have had two teachers who determined the course of his life. They were Hamm, his father and Renn, the servant. Renn knew the land. He took Sostris to the desert's edge and taught him how to snare a rabbit and hunt the quail with a throwing stick. He showed him how to float on a bundle of papyrus stalks, his slim, forked spear ready to flash into the water at an unsuspecting fish. He taught him when to plant. He passed on to Sostris the inherited knowledge of a hundred generations of dwellers on the land.

Hamm knew the gods. His knowledge was vast: he had learned all the tales from his grandparents and the other elders of the region. Sostris worked side by side with his father and Renn, watching, listening, learning. His father would recite the stories as they worked, telling of the kings they served and of the gods from whom the kings were descended. He told of the spirits that inhabited the birds and the animals, the plants, the springs and the cliffs that overlooked his valley.

The tales explained the sun and the stars, even the meaning of life itself. Theirs were gods who commanded love and respect and often fear. They were gods who controlled his life and destiny. Some were benevolent, bringing prosperity and good fortune. Others stalked him with cunning or waited silently to strike unaware with sickness or accident.

After the day's work, Sostris would sit with his father, hearing the tales of Re who travelled daily across the sky in his celestial boat; of Geb, the Earth, who consented to having the river, the rocks and all living creatures upon his back; and of Thoth, the moon, the god of science and wisdom, the measurer of time and lord of numbers.

Hamm saw the interest that Sostris had and told the tales again and again, knowing that his son would be the next link in the unbroken chain that carried the knowledge through the generations.

Sostris learned well, growing to manhood with his gods in his heart and a genius for the land in his mind and hands. He lived within the confines of the river valley, bound to his few acres. He ventured occasionally to the desert's edge, astounded by the meeting of lush farmland and arid waste. He visited the graves of his ancestors bringing simple offerings of bread and beer. He accepted his life, serving well his king and his gods.

He accepted the rhythm of his life, attuning himself to the tempo of his world. The sun, the moon, the river, his fields, all moved with a regularity that said to him: 'This is happening because it is time for it to happen.' His life's pulse beat untiringly through the years. He worked the land, he married. He paid tribute to his unseen king, he joyed at the birth of his son. He buried his father, joyed again at his second son, worshipped his gods.

He took his sons to the fields, showing them the wonders of the land. He told them of the multitude of gods with whom they lived. He watched them as they played together or went with old Renn to the river's shore. With time he gave them a hoe and showed them how to work with the gods to coax life from the rich, brown earth.

The waters had again receded, leaving behind the silt that nourished the land. Sostris worked with his wife and sons, carrying muck from the canals to the patch of grapes and the garden near the low, clay tile house. It was Sostris' thirty-second flood. As the sun neared the western horizon the family went to the house for the evening meal of corn, sun-dried goat meat and figs.

Sostris went out to watch the sun sink behind the tombs of the rich and the simple graves of his father and ancestors. He beckoned to his sons. They came quickly, eager to hear the tales which their father told so well.

Sostris closed his eyes and let the pictures swim in his head. The goddess Nut, the mighty Osiris, Horus the valiant, the dog-headed Anubis, Thoth the wise, all these were as real to him as the sun in the sky and the land beneath his feet. He remembered his father and how he spoke; how his hands reached to the sky then opened out and out, his voice ringing with passion as he told the tales of good and evil, of the gods who who ruled humans' lives.

He opened his eyes and looked across the river. The cliffs were darkening against the western sky, their faces in shadow. He saw the river as it moved patiently, powerfully past. He felt its current flowing in his own blood, the rich smells of the marsh rising to his nostrils on the warm evening air. He saw his sons sitting before him on the ground, their eyes wide, expecting. A great joy filled his heart, a satisfaction with his family, his land, his gods, his life.

"Before this river and this land," he began, the story coming from his lips as he had heard it countless times from his own father, "before the sky, even before Re, there was only a sea. It was wider than a thousand skies and immeasurably deep. A flower appeared upon this ocean and the flower was Re, the sun god. And time began.

"Re created from himself four children: Schu and Tefenet, Geb and Nut, and they all lay with their father upon the great ocean. They created a world with Geb as the land and Nut as the sky, Schu and Tefenet the air and the winds that drifted between heaven and earth.

"From Nut and Geb were born Isis and Osiris, Seth and Nephthys. They roamed across the earth filling it with all the wonders that we know today. The birds in the air, the river with all its creatures, the trees, the rocks, the restless sands of the desert: these are their work and their play.

"But we are their Art! We are their special creation. Like the fish and the birds, the mountains and the sand, we are filled with their life. But in their wisdom the gods gave us an extra gift: the power to see the glory and spirit that they instilled in all their creations."

Sostris was filled with a conviction inspired by the words. An idea came to his mind which he felt compelled to share with his sons. He broke from the generations-old story and added his own words, confident of their truth, certain that they would add to his sons' understanding.

"This is the secret of pleasing the gods," he continued. The boys heard no change. They sat spellbound by voice and gesture. "Each of the gods' creations has a duty to fulfil, a reason for its existence. That duty is to be exactly that what it was created to be. The snake is purely a snake; the reed in the swamp can be naught but a reed; the stone must lie by the field, a stone.

"The bird in the air satisfies the gods with its flight. We discharge our duty when we see with our eyes and feel with our hearts the celestial power that carries the bird on the wind. The same power that carries the bird, that opens the seed, that sends the river past our door lives here in us," he said softly, his hands settling lightly on his breast. "This is our obligation to the gods. We must be what they created us to be: their Art, testimony to their power and their glory."

Sostris returned to the legends of old. He told of greater and lesser gods, of their passions and quarrels, of divine jealousy and monumental wrath. The boys listened engrossed, visions of superhuman deeds dancing before their eyes.

The day was dying, the last light fading in the western sky. Father and sons sat on the earth, feeling the power of their gods around them.

"Tell us again of Osiris, Father," said the older boy.

The gods of the night had assumed the throne; Re had started his journey through the underworld. The darkness was full of secrets but the boys felt no fear. Re had "gone to the west" but would travel on the river that flowed beneath the earth to be reborn with the next dawn. Sostris knew that he and his sons would one day cross the river to dwell in the west as his ancestors had done before him. He too felt no fear. He knew that his gift from the gods, his "Ka" would live on in the land of the dead where Osiris reigned supreme.

"Osiris was a great god, loved by his people, our ancestors. He was a just god. He loved his people and they prospered. He and his sister-wife Isis ruled on earth, loyal to the all-powerful Re.

"Seth, the brother of Osiris, saw the people's love and wanted it for himself. His envy of his brother filled him with hate. With treachery and deception he slew Osiris. But the power of Isis was greater and she worked a mighty spell, restoring life to his limbs. Great though her power was, Osiris could not return to rule over the land. He remained as king in the realm of darkness."

Sostris paused, his zeal coursing through his veins like molten silver, feeding the fire that flared in his heart. Here was the source of his strength, here was his motive power, his reason to be. 'Life is so short,' he thought, catching a glimpse of eternity. He smiled softly, offering a short prayer of thanks to the gods who had granted him the gift of truth.

He told his sons of Osiris' domain. It was a land of freedom from the trials of earthly life. An island of plenty with fields of grain higher than a man can reach awaited the one who had proven himself worthy. The island could only be reached by boat. The ferryman who piloted the boat always looked to the rear observing the conduct of those waiting on shore.

"The rewards are great for him whose life is just. As Osiris lives, so shall he live; as Osiris conquered Death, so shall he not die.

"The door of heaven is unbarred, it stands open before you. Re awaits you there: he takes you by the hand and leads you through the sacred halls of heaven. He sets you upon the throne of Osiris, upon your throne, that you might be master in your domain.

"The servants of the gods stand behind you. The nobles stand before you calling: 'Come, you god. Come, you possessor of Osiris' throne.' Isis speaks with you and Nephthys greets you. The citizens of heaven bow down before you, kissing the ground at your feet. You stand clothed in the figure of Osiris, first among those who dwell in the west. You do as he did: you leave your house behind you, flourishing, your children protected from worries and woes."

Sostris and his sons sat quietly on the ground. The legend of Osiris glowed in their hearts and minds like a beacon in the night. They stayed a while under the stars then made their way into the house to sleep. Tomorrow was another day of work.

THE ARTIST

I spot her from a distance, her white shoes flashing high as she sprints across the grass. She runs not with style nor with grace, but with determination. She scans around as though looking for a specific person or place. As she nears me her eyes fix upon the empty bench beside mine. She runs harder like getting to that bench is all that matters in the world. She slackens her pace, digging her heels in at the last moment, skidding to a stop. She has a jute sack decorated with stars and moons clamped tightly under her arm, its contents bulging against the fabric showing straight, hard lines and sharp corners.

Mouth open, her breath huffing out in short, fast gasps, she drops to her knees before the bench. She plunges her hand into the sack and retrieves a drawing pad and a big, new box of pencil crayons. The flip top flops back, she pulls out a pencil and bends to her work.

She is the picture of an artist immersed in her craft. Already, at perhaps age nine, she has learned the trick of blocking out the world, focusing only on her sketchpad with a critical eye that demands perfection. The subject of her drawing comes from within; she has no need to look up to measure dimension or depth.

She needs no studio, no easel. She is content with any flat surface upon which to lay her pad. Today she's sitting on her heels, the newly cut grass sticking like pieces of green noodles to her faded jeans. The worn wooden bench her drawing table, she's oblivious to the dog walkers, the joggers and the frisbee throwers with whom she shares the park.

Her unbrushed blonde hair is thrown together in a sort of ponytail as if she had had no time to waste on such unimportant matters. Long flaxen wisps trail tickling across her cheeks as she leans to scrutinize a detail on her page. A hurried hand tucks back the distraction as her pale eyebrows pull quickly together in a scowl at the lost moment. The scowl transforms to a squint of concentration as she lifts the pad to study the picture in a new light. With a quick nod of satisfaction she replaces the pencil crayon to its slot in the box.

She carefully surveys the colours in her prized new set: forty needle sharp darts standing rank and file like troops in a rainbow army. Her hand hovers over the reds then plucks a scarlet soldier to obey her commands.

She moves her feet apart and plops to the ground in a position that looks painful for all but yogis and small children. She clutches the pencil in both hands like holding a baseball bat and pulls it in tight against her chest. She arches back, pushing her belly out and cocking her head to one side as she again studies her work. The squint returns, then resolves to a brief, faint smile as she decides her next step. Like a spring released she uncoils from her bent and twisted posture, seating herself on her heels, her back erect.

She sits motionless but for the hand and wrist that control her pencil. Minutes pass before I notice that her hand stands still. She looks long and questioningly at her picture, tipping her head from side to side. She shrugs once then slowly and carefully tears the page from the pad. She lays it face down on the grass beside her as she returns the pencil to the box and stows all her supplies in the sack. She picks up her drawing, slings the bag over her shoulder and walks past me to a garbage can at the end of my bench. She drops it in and continues down the path to the park entrance.

I sit for a few minutes then close my book. I get up and walk towards the garbage can, being careful not to look in as I leave the park.

VERY SLOWLY THROUGH AMERICA

Twenty years ago I took a trip through the States. It couldn't be described as a holiday in the traditional sense of the word because it wasn't a journey which took me somewhere for a few weeks as respite from my daily round. It was a journey which lasted for a full year, and it was on foot. The travelling itself became the daily round.

We've all experienced the urge to get out for a brisk walk to help us with some important decision making. The movement, the fresh air, the aerobics, even the momentary distraction from the question at hand help us to focus and come to that sought decision. Well, I was faced with the BIG question: "What do you want to do with your life?" so, being a confirmed extremist, I figured such a major decision deserved a major walk for proper rumination. I packed the minimum onto my back, left my beloved Kootenays and hitched to the tobacco fields of southern Ontario. It was 1978 and a season of picking at forty bucks a day got me a grubstake which satisfied the folks at the border crossing and which I hoped would last me well into the winter.

I had heard of a thing called the Appalachian Trail in the eastern States; two thousand miles of hiking was just what I had in mind. New Brunswick ushered me into Maine where I headed straight for the trailhead in Baxter State Park. It was my first autumn away from B.C.'s evergreen forests and I was truly impressed with the deciduous splendour of an eastern fall.

The hills and forests of New England are charming in a true sense of the word. Small lakes are not lakes, but rather Ponds, and hiking around them and camping near them quickly made clear to me Thoreau's fascination with and love of his Walden Pond.

I consciously didn't get a copy of the Appalachian Trail guidebook. I chose to inform myself (or not) of what was to come just through contact with locals and other A.T. hikers. I followed the white blaze marks which distinguish that trail from any others for its entirety from Maine to Georgia. I was heading south and in the first hundred or two miles I met many "end to enders" who were approaching their goal with feelings ranging from relief to desperation to premature longing for what had just been. There were casual hikers doing only three or four hundred miles, local strollers and "white blaze purists" who were doing every inch of the trail.

Enjoying natural beauty is of course important, but it wasn't my prime motivation for this trip. I was interested in meeting the people of rural America; the fantastic land and skyscapes were an added perk. I was no purist bent on completing the entire trail. I wasn't averse to side trips to visit towns and villages which the trail bypassed. I even rode my thumb into the Big Apple, stashed my pack at the bus depot and "hiked" for a day in Manhattan, mostly with my head back and my mouth open. Greyhound got me back to the trail somewhere in Virginia or North Carolina.

If you've heard that the Smoky Mountains, a southern chain of the Appalachians, were beautiful, then you heard right. They get their name from the ever-present mists that hang like smoke. It took me a week to get through Smoky National Park, every day of which I still cherish.

There were far too many experiences, human and natural, to touch on them all. It was an unforgettable geography lesson. At the most natural of all travelling speeds, walking, one learns with an intensity which impresses deeply. A full day on a high ridge above the Shenandoah River, passing through nameless impoverished Appalachian villages, a week of trudging through knee-deep crackling leaves and scores of others are impressions which last.

The Appalachians end abruptly. I found myself standing at the south end of that major continental range (our Laurentians are a northern extension) gazing out over the plains of Georgia. It was reminiscent of Saskatchewan with its low horizon and overwhelming sky, but the dirt was red and even from the height I could see that those weren't wheat fields. Simple state maps helped me avoid highways as I walked on backroads past remnants of cotton and peanut harvests. I resisted the temptation to make a nine mile sidetrip to visit Jimmy Carter's hometown and kept walking with my face to the sun and my back to the north.

I barely noticed crossing into Florida: around me was still the same awe-inspiring agricultural dreamland, the people were still just as friendly and hospitable and the drawl still kept me on my toes. To this day I carry images (in my mind, I didn't take a camera) of individual trees which, besides the people, epitomize for me the deep south: oaks with branches the size of a Douglas fir; giant pecans with their fallen fruit lovingly inviting me to fill my foodbag; Australian pines with their segmented, pull-apart-like-horsetail needles; and the coconut palms!

Florida captivated me for three months. I explored both the Gulf of Mexico and the Atlantic coasts as well as that decadent heaven called the Florida Keys. I'll admit, there were days when I swam more than I walked. The oceans there are a wonder: coral reefs beyond your . . . you know the expression; mask and snorkel encounters nose to nose with friendly barracuda; writing a poem to a mangrove tree; the rich social life of the transient community.

Winter came and went and I could feel the Kootenays pulling me back. I stuck to backroads again and made my way across Alabama, Mississippi, Louisiana, Texas, Arkansas, Missouri, Texas again, New Mexico and Arizona, "accepting rides" now and then, mostly offered, sometimes asked for. The contrasts of land are phenomenal; the sameness of the generosity and hospitality in all regions was gratifying. The people in New Orleans are equally as wonderful as those in the Ozarks or the southwestern deserts.

The Grand Canyon was a highlight I must mention. There I truly did want to commune with nature and avoid my fellow humans. I explored the canyon for three days and nights, gaining an inkling of what I think religiosity might be.

Many places, many faces. Sand, snow, pavement, boardwalks, countless main streets, mud. Elation, depression. Rocky peaks, salt flats. I visited thirty states during those nine months of walking and believe me, I could tell you stories.

So if you ever get the urge to travel the U.S., do it. The land and the people are wonderful. And if you're doing it on foot give me a call and I might come with you.